Magdalena Tulli

F · L · A · W

Translated from the Polish by Bill Johnston

archipelago books

Archipelago Books
232 Third St. #A111
Brooklyn, NY 11215
www.archipelagobooks.org

Library of Congress Cataloging-in-Publication Data
Tulli, Magdalena.
[Skaza. English]
Flaw / by Magdalena Tulli ; translated by Bill Johnston. – 1st ed.
p. cm.
ISBN 978-0-9793330-1-9
I. Johnston, Bill, 1960– II. Title.
PG7179.U45S5713 2007
891.8'538–dc22
2007027843

Distributed by Consortium Book Sales and Distribution
www.cbsd.com

Jacket art: Cover of *Everyman* Special Belgian Relief Number,
November 1914, "How the thousands of refugees who entered Antwerp
were fed." Courtesy of the Mortimer Rare Book Room, Smith College.

This publication was made possible with the support of Lannan
Foundation, the Polish Book Institute, the Mary Duke Biddle Foundation,
the National Endowment for the Arts, and the New York State Council
on the Arts, a state agency.

F·L·A·W

FIRST WILL COME THE COSTUMES. THE TAILOR WILL supply them all wholesale. He'll select the designs offhandedly and, with a few snips of the shears, will summon to life a predictable repertoire of gestures. See – scraps of fabric and thread in a circle of light, while all around is darkness. Out of the turmoil will emerge a fold of cloth, the germ of a tuck fastened with a pin. The tuck will create everything else. If it's sufficiently deep, it will call into existence a glittering watch chain on a protruding belly, labored breathing, and a bald head bedewed with perspiration. One thing leads to another. The outward appearance brings with it certain attributes: gluttony, pride, and a disagreeable matter-of-factness that douses every impulse of the heart like cold water poured from a bucket. For each three-piece suit there have to be at least two linen kitchen aprons, one for the lady of the house, one for the maid. But there should only be a single gown, in finest taffeta for example. A second one would spoil everything. The plot would be over before it began, brought to a close by a premature scandal.

As for the maid, a length of flower-patterned calico will suffice for her frock. Half a dozen needlework samplers proclaiming banal and dubious bourgeois truths, and a set of baby linen composed of diapers and clothing – these are too trivial for the tailor to bother with, and besides, they are bound to appear anyway at the appropriate moment, spontaneously, owing their existence to a domestic sewing kit kept in a tin. With them will come all sorts of hopes, expectations, and calculations, and in time, by the very nature of things they'll start to acquire the leaden weight of disenchantment. Where school uniforms are concerned, the tailor's expertise will prove indispensable. But even if the matter is spread out over time, it will still eventually roll to an edge beyond which there will be nothing but disorderly collapse and blasts of failure. The only hope for happy endings lies in shortening the tale – in snapping off the story lines early enough, before they fray and grow impossibly tangled. And above all in avoiding climaxes that, like fire, once started will reduce every hope to ashes.

Things could stop at the tailor if, in a sudden rush of sympathy, he were to decide to spare the world the frenzy of desires and disappointments. He would need only to refuse to collaborate, to decline his advance – to abandon the job and run away, shouting at the top of his voice that all that can be seen does not exist. And everything else? If it exists, it is invisible. It's quite possible the world would still believe only its eyes and ears, believe in the weave of fabrics, in their rustle, in the gleam of buttons.

By night the soft rattle of the sewing machine is heard, and in the morning all will be ready. The tailor's shears impassively cut the cloth and the sateen for the lining. The needle pierces them over and again, drawing with it the thread without which the stitch would be useless. In the display window, next to an immaculate notary with a fur collar, there hangs a finished fraternity student – a shapely jacket with a disquieting emblem pinned to the collar. A rotund maid in a flower pattern, pressed for Sunday, a handful of brand-new airmen in a plausible shade of gray, a policeman in dark blue uniform cloth, a bridegroom black as pitch, and a snow white bride behind a chiffon veil. They are neither bad nor good; given their scant reserves of patience, they've been kept too long in abeyance, away from the scene of the action that is only now about to begin, living on dreams alone. They are strung on wooden hangers, with no ground beneath their feet, with no feet even, till the moment comes for them to take the first step. They are waiting for their time, unaware that their fate has been fulfilled in advance, in the tissue-paper sheets of the patterns.

In one place, for instance, the material has been slightly stretched, while in another it is a little wrinkled; the excess has been folded into the seam and more or less ironed flat, so that the whole, along with the facts, should match long-established conclusions about one or another of the characters. As the first costume at hand is examined, it's hard not to be disagreeably surprised that under the lining, nothing is the way it appears on the surface. Various small defects in the cut will reveal incidentally that the materials have been apportioned unfairly and in short supply. It might be observed that matters of the highest importance are decided by prejudice and whim. But it's easier to be unobservant. Whoever is able, deliberately sticks with his initial impression, refusing to acknowledge anything new. The eye would rather ignore any troubling details. And with even greater providence, it prefers to ignore all details whatsoever. Whoever is able, in such a manner protects from doubt his hopeful notions of the whole – notions that may well be more valuable than the whole itself.

The work of the shears is irreversible, and no alterations can be made. The designs contain the entire truth, both that which it behooves everyone to believe and that which no one can be bothered to check. They offer support for any commonly accepted view. The design is a template for the mass production of opinions. Are not even the most dubious judgments lent credibility by the eloquent clarity of the cut? Each outfit is a sign and a suggestion; each revives antiquated associations and arouses expectations that are not coincidental. And at the same time, from top to bottom, or rather from the crown of the hat to the soles of the shoes, each one defines a posture that even in movement is in its own way unchanging, stubborn, incompatible with anything at all. The costumes do not match one another. Their neutral, muted tones are the best guarantee that on a crowded street they will at least not clash. But color will not reconcile them. Especially overcoats – not when they are completely new, but when they've already been worn for some time and have been marked by their encounter with the rough surface of reality. Then they become the source of undying antagonisms, the cause of unseen tensions and excessive atmospheric pressure, ready to explode like compressed steam, and capable of setting in motion even the most sluggish chain of events. But why should the tailor care about all this as he sews stitch after stitch of gold braid onto a general's collar, his tape measure slung around his neck, his gaze unseeing behind thick eyeglasses? If the plot is on a large scale, it's hard offhand even to list all the items of clothing that will be needed.

And what if I'm the one who placed the order? What if I can barely afford the whole thing? The dozens of packets of buttons for underwear and suits, the countless reels of thread and bolts of cloth? Perhaps the advance paid to the tailor was too small, like an inadequate length of inferior plaid. He alone knows where that mountain of overcoats came from. It's best not to ask. Either it's an overdue job, or he took in additional work on the quiet, so as to come out even. The more perfect the items that sprang from his needle in the first burst of inspired diligence, before the cash was used up to pay the rent, the greater the subsequent shame when things began to descend into the mass production of cheap and poorly made garments. But shame decays; nothing turns to dust faster. It is wiped off with a clothes brush. Discarding his ambitions, the tailor will from now on cut the cloth sparingly and unimaginatively, ever more skeptical, and in the end he'll become sarcastic and malicious, since he can already see that his labor was all in vain. It deserves to be spat upon, nothing more. Whoever pays and calls the shots purchases hours of drudgery over the needle but cannot buy a conscience. The tailor does not feel guilty if contempt soils the costumes. So what if it spatters greasy stains here and there from the oil of the sewing machine, or black drops of bad blood from pricked fingers? Spitting marks fates most painfully, even though saliva leaves no trace.

The needle hurtles unrestrainedly towards its only goal – the final calculation of materials and labor. As the stitches speed up, they'll begin to lose their rhythm and stray from the course indicated by a piece of soap on the dark tracts of fabric. The sleeves of shirts may come out tight; the legs of pants, when they are excessively broad, are always too short, whereas when they are the right width, out of pure mockery their lengths are unequal. Jackets will restrict freedom of movement by creaking at the seams. In time the tailor will come to realize that no item of clothing is returned for alteration. Whoever is paying does not even try the garments on. Whereas the figures for whom this kind of apparel is being made are not important enough here to be able to want or not want anything. Even the worst of the suits will be given to someone; nothing will be thrown away. Then why should the tailor ruin his eyesight over a running stitch when he knows it will never lie well? His angry negligence gives rise to all sorts of problems of appearance, bringing ridicule and humiliation upon those to whom those problems are allotted.

Yet so long as no one knows or wants to know about the crucial significance of the cut, a misfortune befalling any of the characters can only seem an inevitable decree of fate, in its own way even just, consecrated by the obviousness with which it is manifest. It never engenders resistance. As can be seen from a certain distance, the victim of the most brutal events is always some insignificant item of clothing incapable of suffering – let's say, a padded overcoat. Its appearance is hazy, its outline blurred. It can be perceived however one likes, in other words, somewhat inexactly: as one of many details fixed, for instance, in the drab prospect of a city square. All around are rows of apartment buildings a few stories high, a landscape that seems created to be the backdrop for opaque goings-on. A hundred overcoats of this kind, or as many as several thousand, is an inconceivable number. A patch of swirling gray of every possible shade, ineluctably shot through with sadness, overcast as if by clouds, with a presentiment of a shared fate desired by no one.

AND HERE IS THE SQUARE, since it's already been mentioned. With a flower bed in the middle, round as a clock face. Ornamental railings on the balconies and lace curtains in the windows. Small yellow blooms in the flower bed and a yellow sun over the rooftops. The sun is unhurriedly crossing the sky. Though it could also be said that the sun is fixed in place, in a corona of yellow rays, and it's the square that is turning imperceptibly, along with the streets that lead off of it, and the small trees on each corner casting scant shadows on the basalt cobblestones. And while there is so little movement that it's as if there were none at all, it still makes one's head spin without cease. Streetcar tracks glisten beside the curb, and along with it they describe a circle that encloses the space in a double steel hoop whose glare dazzles the eyes.

The place may look like some quiet neighborhood of a large city, where squares of this sort are encountered at every step amid the dense network of streets. But the vast whole to which this fragment belongs is not accessible. On each of the several streets connecting to the square, the pavement comes to an end just beyond the corner. Anyone who unduly trusts the solid look of the basalt cobbles and wishes to go elsewhere will immediately be mired in sandy excavations, amid the blank walls of apartment buildings, under windows drawn in chalk directly onto the plaster. Distant steeples and indistinct towers rise over the roofs and suggest the dimensions of the entirety of which this square is supposedly a part. Yet the whole itself must remain conjecture, as imponderable as accomplished facts or as forecasts of the future. Maintaining its substance and its walls and rooftops multiplied in real space would be impossible for me, and also unnecessary. In the meantime, the streetcar is already moving on its tracks. This will be the zero-line streetcar, the only line there is, and more than sufficient for the needs of a single square. Let the shape of the zero, unhurriedly described, accentuate the extraordinary qualities of the circle, a figure perfectly enclosed, whose whole is encompassed by a continuous line without losing a thing.

It goes without saying that all this carries a price – the pavement, the tracks, the streetcar. Every brick and every roof tile has to be paid for. The actual cost of materials and labor is unknown to the characters. Besides, not one of them would be capable of covering these expenses – not the one who can barely make ends meet, nor the well-to-do character wallowing in the illusion of financial comfort. The banknotes carried in wallets are real only in their own particular way and cannot be used to buy any of the truly meaningful things – costumes, landscapes, or interiors. That which is most important has to be imposed on the characters without any choice. They do not know, and do not wish to know, what it is that I arrange out of their sight. I provide work for painters, upholsterers, and decorators; for mechanics and lighting specialists; for swaggering types with cigarettes permanently stuck in the corners of their mouths; for master craftsmen and apprentices in crumpled overalls who value their pay and despise their work; for devout servants of all their own weaknesses. Were it not for the odious job it is their lot to perform, were it not for the rule in their pocket and the scuffed bandages on their fingers, they would have nothing but the despair that wrenches them from sleep at dawn. They are bound to me as I am bound to them. I pay the advances and swallow without a murmur both smaller and larger chicaneries. I do not question the bills when they include props already long since paid for and used, or repainted backdrops in which a hole from a previous hook gives the game away at once.

How painful it is to see plainly all the shortcomings of this world, its shabbiness and its inability to actually exist. I turn a blind eye to the true state of things. I turn another blind eye and refuse to see anything at all. On principle I cannot abide bringing complaints; I prefer not to say a word if, for instance, all the roofs leak. The people in overalls already believe that they work too hard for such a laughable wage, which buys nothing more than a bare wall. They would greet naïve expectations of professional dedication with a shrug of the shoulders. Dissatisfaction is imprinted on everything they touch. Doing nothing beyond what is habitual and indifferent in their occupation, they award themselves compensation for some alleged wrong – calmly, without expecting anything to be docked from their pay. Whatever they neglect and whatever job they botch, they themselves will not suffer any loss.

Yet the success of the entire undertaking depends to a great extent on its external appearance. It depends on whether the designs will be developed with flair, and whether surfaces can be covered with a patina to suggest, convincingly and deceptively, that the world was not created yesterday – that since time immemorial there have existed the same magnificent elevations, faced, let's say, with granite, and the same stained-glass panes have remained without a single crack in the windows of stair-wells; that the same oak floors glisten with wax, and the same veined marble appears on café tabletops, while engraved brass plates proclaim the ancestral glory of institutions as indestruc-tible as the workings of a gold watch. The crude power of the money expended on materials and labor will always have its effect, but it will not inspire passion. One can buy routine but not a love for detail. Cash will not guarantee a noble equilib-rium of sheen and patina. And if this is not to be had, one must be satisfied with a cheap story that isn't worth the fortune sunk into the construction of its setting. It is no longer possible to count on something truly entrancing.

Inconveniences, like poorly made clothes, when allocated without discussion and without being tried on, become a public sign of disgrace too painful to accept and too intense to simply ignore. The wave of bitterness that rises from disillusion never recedes. And the bitterness, in the form of a chronic anger, circulates in a broad orbit, contaminating thoughts and deeds. There is no answer to the question of how a switchblade found its way into some pocket, or where a set of brass knuckles came from. Moreover, it can be seen at a glance that the knife and the brass knuckles are not fake. They are the real thing, unlike other props such as imitation rings or bouquets of artificial flowers, which are present in abundance. Unlike the cunningly fashioned reproduction marble in different varieties, unlike the high-quality hardwoods made from common timber with the aid of stains and varnishes, these troubling objects are free of the stigma of hole-and-corner economies; the best materials were used in their manufacture.

It is not by chance that no one here, not even the policeman, is allowed to bear arms. I have not ordered any guns; they do not appear in the invoices and are not to be found in the warehouses. Yet revolvers are nevertheless in circulation, in most cases properly cleaned, loaded, and ready for use. They are hidden in dark drawers. Where have they come from? It's obvious they did not originate in the tailor's shop, or even at the carpenter's. And since they exist, they must have been brought by some route. Perhaps these guns have always circulated between stories, passed from hand to hand – smuggled goods, bought under the counter in forbidden regions at the juncture of various tales, in the place where stories interpenetrate, stirred up by their own feverishness. The price of the questionable profits sought by the overall-clad workmen is the despair and rage of the secondary characters. But for various reasons, for as long as possible all is consigned to oblivion, and no one insists on penalties.

I have many motives for yielding, surrendering, for humbling myself in the face of arrogance and unparalleled chicanery – for giving up any idea of scrutiny, quietly acquiescing, accepting false invoices as genuine and paying for fictitious labors and purposely failed jobs planned as alibis for other dealings, under-handed and quietly profitable. A solemn insistence on compar-ing the invoices with the actual state of things will do no good; nor is there any use in longing for the unambiguousness of arithmetic, or a compulsive predilection for bookkeeping. The invoices, for instance, list whole tons of silver nails, the price of which suggests that this specification is quite literal; the expenditure strikes one at once as insanely wasteful, as if these kinds of nails were being required even in the construction of scaffolding made from untreated pine planks. The simple act of counting pallets, boxes, and items disturbs the calm of the warehouses. It provokes the appearance and disappearance of objects as though out of spite, thwarting efforts at invigilation. Because of this, it is impossible to ascertain beyond a doubt whether anything really existed or whether it merely featured in the accounts, like last year's snows, like the first rays of the springtime sun, summer lightning storms, or autumn mists.

Who does it all belong to, and whose property is being stolen? To this straightforward question, which naturally suggests itself – someone has said "I" several times already – there is no hon-est answer. Concealing oneself is exhausting, and in the long run quite impossible. But the word "I" explains nothing here. Alone, it means too little. Less than a signature on a promissory note – no more than a crooked initial left by some hand on a dilapidated wall. This single letter contains so very little that it belongs to everyone and to no one. A vague gesture in the air directing attention to a button at the throat will not add much, yet at the same time it cannot be made any more comprehensible. Even the image of a silhouette in movement, devised from the cut and style of a garment, would merely be a starting point for facile, superficial associations. What do I need all this for? one might ask suspiciously; what's the use of events, or of the tribulations of the characters embroiled in them? In the face of such questions, there is nothing to do but duck, as if dodging a rock hurled from a street corner. If it struck you on the head, it could kill outright. But it will probably miss and only whistle past the ear.

GIVEN THE DIMENSIONS OF THE SQUARE, no more than two stops will be needed. One of them can be located on the north side, the other on the south – the former in front of the local government offices, the latter outside the boys' grammar school. In the deserted space, a character who plainly belongs to the previous day is presently staggering along. His body, taken from goodness knows where, and in its own way utterly without volition, is a perfect match for the cut of the jacket. Even the disdainful glint in his eye is merely the reflection of a dime-store signet ring. He is a student, drunk. He vomits as he holds on to an iron railing. The streetcar he stepped down from is already moving off towards the government offices. Left behind, rolling about under the seats is an abandoned stick

– a handy device for smashing windows. Even if the student flunked his Roman Law exam yesterday, he already managed to forget about it, because afterwards he put his heart and soul into roaming the streets all day with his pals, following which they spent half the night eating, drinking, and brawling in a club. And what if I am that student? My ears are still ringing with the sound of broken glass, while my stomach is convulsed by painful spasms. Though this particular moment is immensely disagreeable, some subsequent one is sure to bring relief. His only regret was losing the stick, which wouldn't have happened but for the crush of gloomy thoughts immediately beneath his diaphragm – thoughts that were easily ingested yet indigestible, and were violently seeking a way out.

Early in the morning, before the clear air fills with the dust and fug of the later hours, the policeman begins his rounds of the square. His footsteps echo. Pigeons flap out of his way and fly off to the ledges of the apartment buildings. The policeman pauses outside the government offices, lifting his head and gazing at the sky as if he were trying to figure out which way the wind was blowing or whether there would be rain in the afternoon. And now the streetcar is coming again. Amid a squeal of brakes it pulls up at the stop outside the offices. A group of airmen emerges – the first wearing what is undoubtedly a general's uniform, the second a major, after the major a captain, and bringing up the rear a young adjutant with the rank of lieutenant. They stand and look about. As they peer down the side streets the major explains something to them, the general shrugs, the captain is upset and has something to say too, while the lieutenant remains silent, looking from one to the other till eventually the major shrugs his shoulders in a gesture of helplessness. There has evidently been a troublesome mistake concerning the coordinates, and perhaps also the calendar: where the hell is the airfield they were supposed to visit, with its hangars, its planes, and its mess hall, in which there would be coffee in gaudy paper cups, a pinball machine with flashing colored lights, and a jukebox playing loud music at the drop of a coin? Something had gotten mixed up in their itinerary, and at this early hour it could not be corrected. Weary and sleepy, they come to a halt in front of a hotel, allow the general to enter first, then disappear in turn through the door.

In the meantime, the streetcar has completed one circuit and is in the middle of another. At the stop in front of the grammar school, a maid is just getting out. She's carrying a basket with vegetables and a chicken to make soup for the notary and his family. It may be that the policeman would gladly have taken the basket and carried it up the kitchen steps for her, especially if he had been younger or in his civilian clothes, but the gravity of his uniform and the fact that he is on duty does not permit it, so he merely snaps his fingers to the shiny peak of his cap. The maid pouts fetchingly and casts him a lingering glance, but she walks on and vanishes into the entranceway at number seven. It makes no difference to her what whole this neighborhood is taken from, of which city it is supposed to be a part. It should be added that the griffin or eagle on the policeman's cap is a miniature of the national emblem from over the entrance to the government offices – one of those numerous predators, white, black, silver, two-headed, or whatever, that are customarily found on the façades of public buildings. Their precise pose and the shape of their talons and wings depend simply on where the story is taking place. The policeman, taken in by the sight of bell towers and steeples in the background, above the rooftops, in the distance, indistinct and so not wholly self-evident, would also be fully entitled to know, would he not? But he never asks, being content with the reassuring sound of the word "hereabouts." The story is not taking place here or there. It fits in its entirety into itself as into a glass globe containing all that is needed for every conceivable eventuality.

The policeman moves on as the streetcar continues its route around the square. How would that rather faded uniform sit on me? Maybe it would pinch under the arms? If I am the policeman, there was a time when I risked my neck in the trenches for the emblem that appears on my cap. Let's say that in my collarbone I bear a memento of the last war – the vestige of a brief and fortuitous instant of unparalleled heroism that can be recounted over a bottle for the rest of my life. On state holidays I pin a medal to my uniform. The fragment of shrapnel makes itself felt with a shooting pain when the weather's about to change, especially if rain is on the way. Still quite handsome,

I grunt in the bathroom every morning. Then, standing in my long johns in front of a cracked mirror, I soap up my cheeks with a shaving brush. I button up my uniform, which after years of service has grown a little tight around the waist. In the evening my wife, a dozen curlers in her hair, fries up some potatoes and pork rinds, griping all the while, and then stokes the stove with more coal since she still has to put the laundry on. The policeman sits on a kitchen stool in his undershirt, his pants rolled up, and soaks his corns in a basin.

At such moments, as if in a dream, through half-closed eyes he sometimes happens to picture the notary's maid and a shudder passes through his entire body. In principle, though, he prefers to reflect on bitter and concrete things – his woefully meager wages, and the promotion that passed him by. The endless tedium of writing reports. Day after day that onerous task is put off till the late evening, and then what? A person is even less inclined to do the job, but there's no getting out of it. His wife, shifting the pots about on the stovetop, has no idea how burdensome it is. The pork rinds sputter in the frying pan, and clouds of smoke fill the kitchen all the way up to the ceiling, which has grown black during all the years they've been married. A coating has accumulated on the painted paneling and the yellowed white of the cabinet doors. Every day it's washed off with a cloth soaked in soapy water. The stale mingled odor of soap and grease lingers in the nooks and crannies. But the policeman is unaware of it, since that is the smell of his entire life.

If I am the notary's maid, on the second floor of the apartment building at number seven I take the vegetables out of the basket and set about making lunch. I'm not attracted to the policeman whatsoever, but it's nice to see how, when he spots me, he pulls in his stomach beneath his tight uniform jacket. In any case, he's too old and he's married. I like someone else: the law student. Peelings fall into a bucket; all at once the knife slips, and blood drips from a cut on her finger. It's nothing serious; it'll heal before her wedding day, as the saying goes. It's all because of the student. Because of his smart jacket, and especially the sweater that he wears underneath on cold days. At the thought of the sweater her heart skips a beat – it's hard to believe wool can be so soft. In the evenings the maid sobs into a wet pillow. She does not get her hopes up. He's always looking the other way when he passes her. And even if he spoke to her, a giggle suppressed by a work-chapped hand would have to suffice for a response. She senses that she knows only words of the lowest quality, those which, like the chicken she is making broth with, have wings that are not made for flight. Other, better words are lacking. What they are, the maid does not know. Something light, easygoing and fanciful, since only words like that can capture the attention of well-dressed bachelors. Words created for eligible young ladies. Beyond a doubt created mostly for them. She would give anything to know what it is that young ladies talk about with the student. Yet she has never seen him with any of them; he's always alone. He would be walking along the sidewalk beneath the windows overlooking the street, while the young ladies were on the illuminated screen in the dark movie theater, in silk dresses, lovely as butterflies.

While the grammar school custodian is cleaning up the mess by the school railings, cursing the unknown drunk who puked on his sidewalk, the policeman stops outside number three, by the window display of the photographic studio, to cast a dreamy glance in its direction as he does every day. Here everything is in its place; in the middle is a large photograph of a woman in a white fur coat. With the passage of years, she has not aged in the slightest and is still just as beautiful and just as unattainable. She looks absently at the policeman from the depths of a different story – one that is black and white but even so is more attractive and more edifying than this one, which matches the color of the yellowing plaster and twines in a crooked knot round the flower bed in the square. The policeman touches the peak of his cap respectfully, then moves on. Aside from the portrait there is nothing dear to him in the window, which is filled entirely with wedding pictures, including one of him and his wife, rather discolored now. The pairs all look alike – a black tailcoat and a white veil. If the veils were separated from the tailcoats and the halves of pictures shuffled, the newlyweds themselves would probably be unable to find their own likenesses in the mass of almost identical figures. Nevertheless the photographer, at this time of the morning closed up in his darkroom, is developing pictures of infants one after another. These prints, paid for in advance and impatiently awaited, bear witness, on the contrary, to the permanence of the order that joins couples together till death, and even beyond.

At this hour the notary, burdened by his own weight and suffering from insomnia, is just getting out of bed. He blows his nose into a white handkerchief, marking it with dark flecks of congealed blood; he brushes his teeth, leaving streaks of red on the porcelain washbasin. Somehow or other a few dark red specks have even managed to appear on the mirror, right in the middle of the reflection of his bald head. A tense and unpleasant grimace twists his mouth as he wipes the mirror clean. He reaches for the shaving brush, then for his razor. In the reflection, his artery pulses beneath his unprotected skin. If I am the notary, I shave with caution, and my hand never trembles. Before my eyes I can still see the blood I just wiped off the mirror, a reminder that my body is tired and all set to lower its tone. To cheer himself up, the notary hums a popular aria from an operetta in a rather pleasant baritone. He has a hope that things will once again return to the way they used to be; against common sense he believes he will never give in. Yet even if capitulation is inevitable, he has no choice but to endure in wordless resistance as long as his strength permits. What else can he do? Nothing but fasten the buttons on his pants, his shirt, his vest. Slip his watch into its pocket and pin the gold chain across his fat belly.

Before he puts on the jacket of the three-piece suit, he ought to ring for the maid and have her bring him his coffee. But instead he himself quietly enters the kitchen. He sees the maid's back as she leans over the table, peeling vegetables. He measures her with his gaze from the threshold, and recalls one by one the women he once used to visit. All were better looking than her, and all better dressed. Secretaries, nightclub singers, wealthy widows of his clients. But that is all gone for good. The notary sighs. He walks up to her and places his hands under her apron and her blouse, no more. In order to allow himself such a caprice in his own home, he has to abandon for a moment his role as respectable lawyer, breadwinner, and paterfamilias – or rather, to take advantage of the fact that the real notary is still suspended on the wooden hanger used for the three-piece suit, blind and deaf, sleeves hanging inertly at each side. The thought of doing something behind the real notary's back always involves a certain risk. At such a moment it's the easiest thing to fall and dislocate one's spine, for instance, and thus for the longest time to be unable to return to the point of departure, where there is simply the glint of a wedding ring as the hand raises a cup of coffee to the lips.

The maid, on the other hand, has no desire whatever to slip out of character, as is quite understandable – she runs the risk of being seriously hurt. So she must pretend that he is not resting his cheek on her shoulder, nor is his hand at the same time groping her body. She has to go on peeling vegetables, oblivious to anything else. He has done this so many times that the situation has begun to seem quite safe to her. It should be added that from the notary's perspective, it would have been foolish not to touch her after he had moved so close. Yet at the same time he knows that nothing else is left for him. Tired right from the start of the day, he longs to feel the beating of his own heart, if only for a second, since he's obliged to gather his strength and head out once again to his office, where he will resume the trivial little procedures that his profession requires. If the notary is to hold up the sky of shared quotidianness, he unquestionably deserves a pillar that can help to keep him in place with his burden.

Thus the maid, whose own future is uncertain, in secret from the notary's wife has to support him beyond the scope of her daily duties, and not without sacrifices on her part. It is on her that the responsibility for the fate of his office, staff, and family will ultimately fall. If his practice fails, the maid will also find herself on the sidewalk – that much is obvious. If this happens, she will have only herself to blame. But in the first instance more important things are at stake. It is not about her, nor about the paralegals and stenographers, but the family. It is about the notary's wife, who this morning has been sleeping off yesterday's migraine, though truth be told for many years now she has rarely gotten up in the morning, and when she has it is only to drift about the apartment in her dressing gown. It is about the boy, fifteen years old, who is at the nearby grammar school and has just been called to the blackboard in his Latin class – lex, legis, and so on – and once again has failed to do his homework, idler that he is. And lastly it's about the little girl, who at this moment is toddling down the hallway, the laces of her tiny shoes untied.

If she tripped over the laces and fell, she would bump her forehead and raise a hue and cry; and if in addition she woke her mother with the noise, it goes without saying that it would be the maid's fault, which goes to show that the maid was responsible for all unforeseen circumstances, against her wishes teetering constantly on the brink of danger whatever course of action she chose, though, on the other hand, she was never allowed to make any decisions of her own accord. Certain of her duties cannot be reconciled with certain others; she cannot simultaneously look after the notary, the little girl, and herself. The simplest thing is to exclude herself right from the beginning, to forget about herself; this no one forbids her, and it would be one less thing to worry about. But both of the other two have their own needs, which cannot at any cost be ignored. Whichever of these needs she attends to, she will neglect others, and so one way or another she won't have a leg to stand on. No one will release the maid from the contradictions inherent in the demands of the master and mistress; neither of them, and even less their children, will resolve these complications for her. From the power and influence that have fallen to the lot of the notary, there follow certain privileges; it is easier for him than for anyone else to shift his cares to someone else's back. His example encourages others to do the same as far as they are able. It is a rule in this story that the weaker person carries the greater burden. Thus, the weakest of all bears everything.

On the other hand, that is after all what they pay her for – to take the entire load upon herself, relinquishing all rights, accepting the brunt of her mistress's anger without a word of complaint, taking on her own shoulders the weight of that lady's unhappiness and disappointments. It's obvious that she is not paid for peeling vegetables – the very idea of such extravagance is laughable. Cooking, cleaning, and ironing shirts seems a natural addendum to the whole, tasks assigned without emotion and without additional compensation. Peeling vegetables for her employers, she secretly asks herself the painful question of why it was not given to her to be someone else. In fact, it's understandable that this question rankles; it was added like a label to the bolt of linen from which her apron was made. But there will be no answer. A maid is a maid, a wife a wife, and that's an end of it. The costume creates the character and takes it into possession, never the other way round.

If things are to move forward, a sign marking the notary's practice should be looked for. It ought to be a brass plate visible from far off, gleaming like gold, engraved with an appropriate inscription indicating to all passers-by, whether or not they need to know, the place where the paralegals are at work – inspiring confidence with their immaculate white shirts and their black oversleeves worn shiny from use; bustling about, utterly engrossed in their pressing paperwork; sprawling at their desks, smoking one cigarette after another, constantly reaching for the telephone. But the signplate showing the place where this establishment is supposedly located is nowhere to be seen. It is neither here nor over there; it does not appear on any of the buildings. Neither at number seven, where the notary's private apartment is located, nor at number one, where there is a café. At number three the photographer has his studio and apartment; at number eleven is the pharmacy, where they know everyone's aches and pains. At number nine the work-weary policeman lives on the back courtyard; while at number five the student rents a cramped little room in the attic. At number eight the washerwoman is cooped up in the basement with a washtub in which someone else's underwear is always soaking in soapy water. At number two there is the bakery, and at number four the movie theater, though it has been closed down and the building in which it was housed is up for renovation; in the meantime, a spare set of keys is kept in neighborly fashion by the photographer at number three, in a drawer beneath a pile of unclaimed pictures. And the hotel at number ten? It's inexpensive but quite decent, just right for middle level businesspeople. It goes without saying that if the notary's signplate were to appear at all, any address would be good, except for numbers six and twelve, where the boys' grammar school and the local government offices stand facing each other. Then what has happened to the plate? It seems that out of forgetfulness, or perhaps deliberately, it has not been put up at all.

What an unpleasant surprise, what an inconvenience and cause for consternation! Of course, the lack of a sign does not necessarily mean the annihilation of the office. It is assumed to have existed since time immemorial, at the very least since when the notary married his boss's somewhat unstable daughter, in this manner becoming a partner. His father-in-law's funeral was magnificent, and the procession started precisely from in front of the office. It's just that it is hard to point the place out. Without a signplate, the office still continues to exist in its discreet fashion, hovering noncommittally somewhere in space, as a putative background for the vest with the gold watch chain and the overcoat with the fur collar, which the youngest paralegal is obliged to take deferentially from his employer when he appears in the doorway. Insofar as the door was ever hung in its frame; insofar as there was even a frame. It's impossible to keep it a secret from the men in overalls that accomplished facts almost immediately become immaterial, which in their eyes renders preparatory labors futile and encourages furtive economies. And it is only thanks to such economies that their work turns out to be so extraordinarily profitable. In their nonchalance, they had been certain ahead of time that the office would not be needed; now they find themselves in a bind. It's too late to repair the mistake. There arises the worry that they will try instead to derail the story to cause it to bypass the office along with its costly and toilsome interior decorations. For the most mundane reasons, this establishment will remain what it is – a hazy notion.

But if I am the notary, this is not my concern. One way or the other I don't like to be late, so now I have to leave home. I have good reason to hurry from the apartment building at number seven. I'm escaping tears and shouts, cold compresses, rows over the little girl's untied shoelaces; getting as far away as possible from my wife's despair and fury, and especially from the maid's unspoken complaints. The enjoyment of drinking one's morning coffee in peace and quiet has proved unattainable in such circumstances, as the notary finally came to understand when he glanced into the kitchen before leaving. The maid, who had just been slapped by her mistress for her unforgivable negligence, was still sobbing as she prepared the chicken for the soup. If I am the notary, I'm angered by the quite extraordinary insolence concealed in her meek, teary-eyed gaze. What do you want from me? I'm already buried under a mountain of problems so much more important than the ridiculous wrong you've suffered. He knew where to go to ensure that even in such troublesome circumstances he did not have to start work without first drinking a cup of coffee – he was familiar with the café at number one. Though in fact, even if he himself does not see it clearly enough, he cannot start work at all. Characters generally have the sense that their future is by the nature of things uncertain. Each mention of going somewhere is by the nature of things shrouded in a mist of indefiniteness, which in itself is not an obstacle. After all, it also gathers in places where there is talk of things past. So if someone decides confidently to call by someplace for a moment or plans where they will go afterwards, they have to count on surprises. Until that moment comes, the future can be imagined any way one likes. The gaze will not search ahead of time for the locations that are being prepared. What has been disregarded on the quiet is not in evidence. Even if what has been disregarded is the most important thing, no decision or design lies behind this fact. It's always just a tangled matter of falsified invoices and furtively acquired goods.

Those carrying out the work would prefer to confess to simple inattention, at most to having neglected their duties, rather than to intentional abuses. Yet if their indolence is the sole cause of their mishap with the notary's office, where the hell have they put the safe in which the deposits were kept? The title deeds of several local buildings, promissory notes of various kinds, even boxes of jewelry? And above all government bonds, larger or smaller bundles of which were surely secured there for various local families. The absence of the safe has come to the fore now, and it's hard to ignore. It goes without saying that they did not place it in the notary's apartment at number seven. Where is it then? What have they done with it? Why have they hidden it? Were they intending to smash open the combination lock? Unceremoniously burn a hole in the armor-plated door with a blowtorch? I can no longer look on with forbearance at this scandalous disappearance. It needs to be said – loudly and clearly, so the master craftsmen and apprentices hear – that the safe must be found.

Yet in the meantime, in accordance with the plan the dark gray notary made of pure wool leaves the entranceway of number seven and heads off to work. The notary is cold; he has problems with his circulation, which is understandable given his weight. His fur collar, standing out proudly amid light autumn overcoats, inspires confidence, as does his profession. The image of the office remains vivid and sharp in his mind, unsullied by any doubt. Even the question of how he is to get there does not cause him any unease. The same way I do every day, he would reply, surprised that it is not obvious. By the streetcar. In his memory he retains the entire past that has fallen to his lot along with the somber three-piece suit and the gold watch chain, so how on earth could he forget his daily ride on the streetcar? As he passes the concierge, who crumples his cap in his hands, he will tip his hat absently, because he is polite even when distracted. He completes his short route unhurriedly and sits at last at a marble-topped table. Just for a moment. He places his order and picks up the daily paper. Yet luckily things will fall out in such a way that before the cup of coffee and the cream cake taken straight from the glass-fronted display case are brought to his favorite table in the corner, he will be called to the telephone. Otherwise he would have had to sink his teeth into the rock-hard rosette of whipped cream crowning a cake made of plaster. And though he is a serious fellow, responsible for home and office, for his staff, his family, and his servants, it would have crossed his mind at that moment that in reality there is nothing for him. Such an extravagant thought is in keeping neither with his vest nor with the dark gray overcoat the waiter took from him a moment ago. Over the fur collar there was no exchange of glances. In this way the two men mutually confirmed their understanding of the order of things; as the notary handed the waiter his coat and hat, with an impatient gesture he hung his umbrella over the other man's arm as if it had been a coat hook, while the waiter's gaze clung humbly to the garments with which he had been entrusted. Though in fact this is of no consequence, and it could even be anticipated that no more attention whatsoever will be paid to the waiter. If at this point someone wanted to exclude the notary's office from events, they would first have to cause the notary himself to diminish in importance. To stop him being in command of this and other situations. Considering his social position and his presumed extensive network of professional and personal connections, it would seem at first glance that such a thing is quite impossible. And indeed it would not be easy to bring about. Whoever undertook it would be obliged to disturb the deepest foundations on which public order is based.

But those responsible for the petty abuses will stop at nothing; they use any method they can to avoid the catastrophe of being discovered, regarding every other kind of catastrophe as a lesser evil. The workmen in their overalls, accustomed to impunity and seeing it without any unnecessary qualms as an encouragement to continue their familiar machinations, are not held back by anything. Those disposing of the misappropriated materials are aware that a crash will level all the old accounts. When it has passed, they'll be able to return to their underhand dealings with a clean balance sheet. Yet in bringing about such a disaster it will not be possible to avoid damage. This is a moment of danger for everyone, including them, the masters and apprentices, because they run the risk of leaving some incriminating trace, some incontrovertible proof of their having acted in bad faith. The steps they were obliged to take to deprive the problematic notary's office of its raison d'être will turn out to be an act of sabotage. Nor would it be the first. No story has ever managed to be played out properly to its conclusion. Yet even if the matter were to be revealed, they will not give up so easily. They'll issue unimpeachable affidavits for one another and write appeals, sticking to their version till the bitter end; they'll try any stratagem, from tears to threats, aware that whatever happens there is no one who could take over their duties.

The telephone in the café will ring for the first time no later than a quarter after ten. It's the notary's wife. His broker called, she informs him resentfully, complaining that her head is splitting. In his view, her migraine is a trifling matter next to the serious problems portended by the message she is relaying. The notary listens, asks a question, and listens some more. His voice sounds calm, but his eyes dart about with increasing rapidity. The phone call from the broker has set him on edge, though it's entirely possible that his wife has gotten the whole thing mixed up. It's easy to check – all he has to do is reach for the receiver he just replaced on its hook. But the broker's number is permanently busy. The notary calls his own office. It goes without saying that he won't get through; he won't even hear a busy signal, as if at the other end of the line there were no telephone, no receiver, and no hand to pick it up. The only thing left for him is the café table, to which he could easily return. But his appetite has abandoned him.

In the opposite corner of the room, the student is leafing through the local newspaper in search of anything he can find about the disturbances whose recent memory fills him with pride. The fracas blew like a storm through the central districts of the city, passing by at a distance the glass display case containing the cakes and sparing it. No one here saw these disturbances, and thus they had as much meaning as the notary's office, about which it can only be said that somewhere or other it probably exists. The memory of the affray fell to the student's lot, along with the metal emblem pinned to his lapel. Without confirmation in the form of broken glass crunching underfoot, without store windows boarded up to deter looting, accomplished facts carried little value. To become reality, they needed suitably dramatic descriptions and the necessary lofty tone. Anger is a symptom of distress and so requires pathos.

But whose distress are we talking about? This question might be asked by the owners of the broken windows, who know only their own worries, because after all they are the ones who will pay for new windowpanes. The answer is precisely the distress that comes from overly tight sleeves, seams digging into tender flesh, pants that are too short, a frayed buttonhole. But when the towering wave of anger comes along, among those it sweeps away there are always a handful of well-dressed figures. The wave will lift up highest of all precisely those whom fate has favored from the beginning. Those whose jackets lie on them as if custom-made, and whose underwear even is no disgrace. Unencumbered by the comicality that blights the lives of many, the student is at ease in his jacket with the emblem pinned to the lapel. Unfortunately though, his pride is tinged with bitterness. More could be explained by a family photograph. To understand what it was all about, it would suffice to notice the hang of his father's cheap Sunday suit. His upbringing was patriotic but his soups were watery, and for supper it was bread and jam. One should also know about the pain of humiliation when, before the honest gaze of steel gray eyes the color of the best lamb's-wool sweater, the more imposing doors slam shut.

If I am the student, I believe that what's needed is to abandon unnecessary scruples and to strike at whatever is unshapely and badly made; it should be swept away and burned without so much as a by-your-leave, so as to bring order. And also to restore the world's pure glow, by the light of which the virtues of true perfection will finally be able to shine. In the meantime, consoled by a mug of beer on an empty stomach and reasonably satisfied with the newspaper reports, whose tone has the strained quality of breaking glass, he ordered bacon and eggs for breakfast. He belched once and twice, and the remainder of the thoughts that had previously lain heavy on his stomach were given release. Rising over the table, they acquired the agreeable silkiness of cigarette smoke. On one side of the student was the notary, whose thoughts to the contrary dropped heavily to the floor, where they snaked about beneath the tables. On the other side, his head empty, sat the photographer who owned the studio across the square. He was drumming his fingers on the tabletop and staring at the outdoor space crammed into the rectangle of the window frame like a thin and slightly dusty white passe-partout. He was frowning and narrowing his eyes. The city landscape outside the window, it seemed, still lacked sufficient depth of field.

Meanwhile, the matter that just a moment before had caused so much disquiet made itself felt again: the phone rang a second time. In the conversation with the broker few words were exchanged, and on the notary's end these were mostly monosyllables. The subject of the conversation was a sudden drop in stock prices across the board, while the Swiss franc had moved decidedly upward. The cause was a political crisis of a catastrophic nature; this was last-minute news too recent to be in the morning papers. The higher the Swiss franc rose, the less was paid for the banknotes in rainbow colors that were the national currency and that one ought to stick with out of a sense of patriotic duty. The trading tables, however, indicated that everyone was racing to get rid of them. And this was only the beginning. In the next couple of hours all the prices on the stock market, including those of real estate, threatened to collapse. It would be the kind of event succinctly known as a crash. This most unpleasant-sounding word was repeated twice. Though of course conditionally, without absolute certainty. Then what shall we do? Shall we sell or shall we hold out awhile, counting on a recovery? This question, on the face of it extremely simple, forced a hurried choice between hope and common sense. It was not easy to deliver the answer. The notary cleared his throat twice before he bid farewell to hope and made all the sensible decisions. Afterwards, he wiped his forehead with a handker- chief and stared unseeingly into space.

In the passe-partout of the window, images of confusion appeared. Passers-by were carrying loops of sausage, slabs of bacon, and sacks of flour or sugar or potatoes. Their eyes glistened. Here and there, groups of grammar school boys elbowed their way through, the same unhealthy gleam in their eyes; because of the unusual political situation, they had been sent home. The notary's son was among them; he came briefly into view in the crowd, right in front of the café window. Drifting with the flow, his glasses misted over, he swept by and vanished, already hidden by those following behind. Above the noise of the street, which was louder than usual and swelling like a fever, there rose the hoarse voice of a newsboy, and the first copies of a special edition appeared in people's hands. The waiter was sent out for the paper; before he returned, the piercing yelp of a dog was heard, and a police whistle rent the air. The newsboy – a teenager in short pants who was the son of the washerwoman – shot out of the throng and fled as fast as his legs would carry him, though no one was chasing him. But the conundrum of these events was nothing compared to the conundrum of the general situation; the contents of the special edition of the newspaper, which the waiter finally deposited on each of three tables, seemed incomprehensible.

Even when the three guests read the headlines to one another across the café, things were scarcely any clearer. The analyses printed in the paper were fraught with contradictions. And since everything had been turned upside down, the waiter permitted himself in a lisping voice to add his two humble cents' worth to the brief dialogue that developed among the tables, because he knew he was not the loser here. In his pocket he had some loose change – to be precise, three coins he had been given by the guests and had kept for himself, pleased that in the general confusion he had gotten the newspapers for free. Determined above all to look after number one, he was counting on being given the day off: any minute now the proprietor would call and tell him to close the café for the day. The student too seemed to be observing the commotion on the square through the window of the café. In fact, though, he was looking higher up, gazing over the throng at the still sky, which was a promising blue without a single cloud.

An icy chill on the back of the notary's neck reminded him it was too late for anything now. His skin prickled, and a moment later he felt a pain in the vicinity of his heart. So he returned home, dragging his feet. On the stairs he stopped at every few steps and clung tightly to the balustrade. When he finally made it to the second floor, he ought to have said at least a word to his alarmed wife. But he lacked the strength; he merely took a wad of banknotes from his wallet and ordered the maid to stockpile supplies. Then, for the longest time he fiddled with the dials of the radio. Other than commentaries from far off in foreign languages, eloquent and uninformative, he found nothing but hissing and crackling. If I am the notary, by now everything has started to bother me. My shoes pinch, my collar chafes against my neck, and the daylight dazzles me. I pull down the blinds and turn on the night-light. The new turn of events, which might have seemed unexpected, had in fact for weeks and even months been in the background as an unpalatable but likely possibility. As frequently happens, life had gone calmly on, right alongside a particularly ominous eventuality. If it only failed to materialize as fact, the cost of precautionary steps taken against it would afterwards seem excessive, and the immoderate, pathetic decisions made by the notary would be said to have been driven by panic. Yet what if, on the contrary, with the passage of time it transpires that the greatest and most unforgivable error was a lack of caution? Whatever course of action one takes, one always emerges either a spineless prevaricator safeguarding himself from the worst or an irresponsible risk taker; it's terribly hard to avoid extremes, not because of a person's own nature but because life is so poorly balanced. The burden of responsibility for the well-being of oneself and one's family is the burden of questions without answers. It all arises from the fact that in matters of the greatest weight, only guessing is possible. Up till yesterday certain special ways out were still available; certain loopholes were still open for those most worried. Now, however, they have suddenly been closed, slamming shut all at once with a thud. And in this way the notary and his family have found themselves in a trap.

The student lay impassively on the made-up bed in his cramped attic, smoking a cigarette and blowing perfect pale blue smoke rings towards the ceiling. He too had a radio and was hearing the same hissing and crackling, but in his view it seemed perfectly natural and indicated a desirable turn of events. Having just finished a substantial breakfast, he was not worried about flour or sugar; he gazed at the clear sky through the skylight, confident that he would also be able to eat his fill in the future, which only now was starting to be truly promising.

The student must have had a sense that whatever awaited others, the thread of his own story would find itself on top, like a strong cord just right for tying all the rest into a bundle.

Foodstuffs quickly ran out in the local stores. With the help of the concierge, the notary's maid carried home the last sack of flour, a hundredweight of potatoes, and a slab of lard. For those who had not been quick enough, a black market sprang readily into being with all its extortionate prices. The props that ended up there, all those extra, previously unanticipated sacks of flour and sugar, were prepared in haste, as it were, under pressure of circumstances that were getting out of hand. Those whose job it was to fill the sacks hurriedly reached for plaster and sand, this time in wholesale quantities, in the hope that before the truth emerged, subsequent events would render it unimportant.

The notary asks himself why he failed for so long to take any action, since he was one of those most alarmed. His heart utterly refuses to obey him, now faltering, now pounding away. Why had he not gotten rid of those damned government bonds in time, even at a loss? Why had he not closed up his practice, placed his capital in Swiss francs, and liquidated ahead of time the apartment on the second floor of number seven? He's already managed to forget certain crucial circumstances, and so he is unable to comprehend how, as one who bears responsibility for the welfare of his family and for his children's future, he could have permitted himself such a risky delay when he knew all along what needed to be done. He never intended to flee to the frozen north, rather to the warm south. And it all came to nothing precisely because he would have had to order a lightweight, bright-colored suit suitable for a lightweight life in bright southern lands. He put the whole matter off till later, until the time when in the place of the movie theater they would open a new fashion store with off-the-rack clothing. The local inhabitants did not understand that this was not possible. If it had been permissible to choose one's attire according to one's own preferences, to be one thing or another as one wished, the story would have fallen apart the moment it began.

As early as ten fifteen, when he took the first telephone call in the café, the notary was asking himself why life was so hard. Hard, and at the same time without meaning, and furthermore cruel, because carrying its weight served no purpose. Since it was without meaning, why could it not be made easier? The notary sensed that the moment was approaching when he would be forced to accept conditions of surrender, and would cease wiping flecks of blood from the bathroom mirror. It was only desires, like half-crazed soldiers assigned to an impossible position by a staff error, that were resisting the invincible forces of inertia, when the whole rest of the army was in retreat.

The suit jacket is already back on the wooden hanger, its sleeves hanging limply at its sides. The notary pulls off his shoes and his necktie. In this manner his office moves further away and vanishes for good. He has just remembered something and has rung for the maid. He wants to know if his son has come back home. He has not. And what about his wife, is she up yet? She's sitting by the window in her dressing gown, watching out for their son, from time to time wiping the steamed-up window with her handkerchief, as if the mist from her own breath were keeping him from view. His wife is being overly dramatic, so the notary believes. The boy has long outgrown his soft cotton baby clothes, and now he needs his independence so as not to become a victim of fate. If I am the notary, in times long gone I too became the victim of fate, for no more profound reason than the softness of cotton and the cut of clothing that my mother continued to regard as suitable when even younger children were dressed in a more grown-up fashion. The memory of that ancient embarrassment, like other memories, was assigned to the notary along with his top-quality wardrobe; it was sewn into it like the stiffener in a shirt collar. Unfortunately, it always reemerges at the sight of his son with his round glasses and his hesitant smile. It does not make the wielding of paternal authority any the easier. Bringing up a little girl is a lot more enjoyable.

So what is the girl up to? She's fallen asleep on the sofa in the living room, tired after a long cry. For some unknown reason, the maid delivered this information in a disagreeable and resentful tone before returning to her work. To minding the pots. To the personals in last week's newspaper. She reads them furtively, ready at any moment to hide the paper from her mistress. She's ashamed of wanting a better fate for herself. Her eyes swollen, she struggles through the tiny print, her index finger pushing the sluggish syllables along. She would get married at the drop of a hat, before dinner even. She would leave the pots on the stove – let them burn. The miraculously acquired provisions, gotten by dint of long waits in long lines, she would abandon just like that, leaving them where they lay in the pantry. She's had enough of the life that fell to her lot along with the linen apron. There's no lack of lawyers. They don't have to be notaries. Some are judges; others, more handsome, are attorneys. She doesn't aim so high; in the columns of advertisements, she's looking, for example, for a sign from a modest law clerk who doesn't have to be well off. He needs only to be seeking an honest and thrifty partner; prosperity will follow in due course. The maid forgets too easily that she is lacking the most important thing: the right costume, which is indispensable if her fate is to change.

Could she possibly be sobbing again? No, she's not the one who is crying. It's the washerwoman's son, the newsboy, in his hiding place on the roof of the building at the back of the courtyard. He too is evidently having a hard time, though like anyone he only wants what's best for himself. The less significant someone is, the more unseemly their self-love appears to all those around them. But even the scrawny mongrel who slinks along by the wall and lives on scraps – even he brazenly wishes for the tastiest morsels for himself. He does not value his miserable life so very much as to hold back always in fear of the stick. Just an hour ago he managed to get hold of a loop of sausage and gulp it down on the spot. And if someone promptly let him have it with a walking stick, it wasn't to rectify the damage, because it was too late for that, but rather out of the natural exasperation that second-rate figures can cause by the very fact of possessing their own will and their own desires.

Scuttling away with a yelp, the mongrel accidentally tripped the newsboy. The papers went flying in front of the entrance to the local government offices at the very moment when the clerks were stampeding out of the building. Nothing could have stopped them. They were not in the least afraid of their director, especially since he had been the first to abandon his duties – he hadn't been seen in the office all morning. The washerwoman's boy tumbled to the ground along with the newspapers. His cap fell off; a handful of coins and two or three battered cigarettes fell out of one pocket, a prized penknife and a large bolt for fastening streetcar rails out of the other. The cigarettes were trampled underfoot, and the penknife vanished instantly. The boldface news headline under the banner, ending in an exclamation point, immediately attracted attention. The government clerks picked up the soiled papers, some bearing heel marks. The newsboy's knees were bruised and grazed. He took a long while getting up; during this time his newspapers disappeared just like his penknife, and his money went missing. While one coin rolled across the pavement and fell into a crack, another came to a stop under someone's boot; there was no sign what-soever of his wares. The passers-by were wrapped up in their own affairs and may not have noticed the newsboy's fall, but they would not have ignored a coin without an owner; their very consciences would have made them bend down and pick it up. All this took place very quickly. Before the newsboy knew what was happening, he was out of business. A moment earlier he had been standing in the middle of the crowd, jostled on all sides, wiping his nose on his sleeve. If I am the policeman, there's nothing more for me to do here, and I can simply stand at the street corner in my ill-fitting uniform and watch the inci-dent with an absent stare. Yet if I am the newsboy, I'm going to have to pay for those newspapers – to hand over the last pennies that down in the basement of number eight my mother takes out of a worn purse which has seen better times. While he is still stunned by the accident, it's hard to predict whether his dismay will spill like oil from an overturned lamp and explode in flames of anger, scattered embers of which are always aglow here and there. The newsboy, sore from his fall and robbed by those more respectable than himself, was still stifling his tears yet already in the throes of a powerless rage. He was still in pos-session of the large bolt from a streetcar rail and would gladly have made use of it, for instance hurling it at one of the win-dows of the government offices.

The policeman's official diligence has its limits: it's possible he would close an eye and pretend not to have seen such an act. In fact, considering the extent of the disturbances already alluded to, present here in the form of newspaper accounts, the sound of one smashed windowpane would be an inadequate finale. Even a dozen broken windows would have meant equally little. Then let's say that the bolt hit the national emblem mounted over the entrance to the government offices. The sharp sound of a police whistle would confirm such a turn of events. As will become apparent at once, the emblem was not made of real metal; proof could be seen in the shards of gilded plaster strewn across the sidewalk, the crown knocked off along with the head, the beak elsewhere. Since it's come to the destruction of a symbol, the same one for which the policeman once risked his neck in the trenches, the offense will prove to be a lot more serious. In such a case the boy would have to be dragged by the ear straight to his mother, the washerwoman at number eight. Let her sign the police report and pay a fine; if she doesn't have the cash, let her borrow it from a neighbor. When the news-boy pulls free and runs away, the policeman will not give chase. He'll promise himself through gritted teeth that he will not let this go unresolved. No kinder solution will be possible.

The clamor and confusion were nothing but a distant echo – and only one of many – of a catastrophic upheaval that was the start of all the troubles. Without it there would have been no political crisis, no crash or subsequent panic. Yet this upheaval could neither be seen nor heard; there was not a word about it in the papers. This is because it took place beyond the circle of the streetcar rails, beyond the ring of buildings that the eye could trace, in the marshaling yards used only by the workers in overalls. There the eardrums of the masters and apprentices were almost bursting.

AMID THE OMINOUS TURMOIL, which rings with nothing but false notes, I don't need to listen intently, or even to guess, in order to know only too well what has happened. With eyes closed one could tell that the catastrophe was brought about by the machinations of those who have too much to hide. Without ever having seen those supposedly abandoned warehouses, the breeding ground of shady business, one could predict every element from the masonry to the roof tiles and not be wrong in a single detail. Hence the walls of blackened red brick and the permanently unwashed windows coated in gray industrial grime. Even if the occasional one is missing its glass, any pale ray of light will still be instantly swallowed up in the dust-clogged air. Electric bulbs glow dimly, powered by current that has been diverted here illegally; in the gloom they barely illuminate piles of cardboard boxes, wooden crates, and burlap sacks. Nor is there any need to open these packages to know what they contain: bars of brass for engraved nameplates, lengths of genuine mahogany veneer, real marble tops for café tables, and even window frames and copper plate for sills. Underneath are heavy cases with the familiar silver nails, unimaginable quantities of which keep being listed, though later on it's impossible to find out what they have been used for. The scale of the undertaking has evidently warranted the surreptitious addition of a narrow-gauge rail line. The siding cuts among the filthy shops, making it easier for the men in overalls to transport the goods that have been put into a second, illicit circulation among stories. It's thanks to the small freight cars that a feverish trade has arisen, the culminating success of which will be a pure profit distilled from the turnover – bottles of untaxed alcohol locked up somewhere in a storeroom. It is a certain thing that at the moment of the great crash, the shops too shook to their foundations. It's even possible that the odd bottle broke; yet all the others survived, packed in cases in their dozens.

The tremor was accompanied by the ringing laughter of the masters and apprentices. The object hurled from high up with such a din was not even a homemade bomb. Rather, it had the weight and dimensions of the missing safe – exactly those, to a T. Yet it struck precisely at the solar plexus of the infrastructure, at the underground bunker hidden beneath the turf, in which the valve of a gas tank used for heating was right next to some electrical equipment and the compressor of an air-conditioning unit. As a result a hole was smashed in the ceiling, a transformer was crushed, and several pipes burst. The series of electrical discharges had catastrophic consequences, though, as had been planned, the far-reaching impact of the subterranean explosion did not affect the red-brick warehouses. The shocks traveled far, perhaps along the water lines. Whoever conceived the plan probably supervised the operation in person. Not alone but in the company of the overalled workmen, who made off-hand comments on the course of events, detecting from the color of the smoke and the sound of the explosions that the compressor alone must by some miracle have survived. In that case, they joked, instead of heating there'd be cooling. As they spoke, bandying strong words, they drew on filterless cigarettes and spat out shreds of tobacco. With a malicious pleasure they applauded the echoes of a disaster that demolished their own labors. Nothing captures hearts and minds quite like the monumental ebullience of destruction. Effortlessly multiplying the losses of the owner and employer, they gave him an appropriate seeing-off: let him regret not sitting quietly while everything except the safe was still in its place. As for me – because I was the one the safe belonged to – it was true that I began to regret things at once.

A discreet silence would at least have made it possible to spare the installations, the buildings, and the pavements. What can be better than silence when truth leads nowhere? The masters have common sense enough not to expect me to believe in their good intentions. But they don't give a hoot; they're not in the least afraid, since they're satisfied that once again they've succeeded in not giving themselves away. After all, didn't the safe appear again at once, though empty? Did they not offer the required show of goodwill, eloquent expressions of false earnestness that for the sake of balance they must have laughed at in private? In the cross fire of questions, one after another of them would have presented his explanations, hesitating and stammering like would-be polyglots who only out of necessity are speaking in a foreign tongue. They would have maintained with hand on heart that the safe had been left in one of the warehouses by a simple oversight; that they had suspended it on the arm of a crane for the sole purpose of installing it in its rightful place without delay; and that everything that happened subsequently was a regrettable accident which was no one's fault. As they were prepared to testify, the reinforced door was opened by the impact of the fall, and its contents, in their view, were swept away by the wind. It all scattered, no one knows where to: title deeds to local apartment buildings in the names of various clients of the photographer or parents of one or another grammar school pupil; certificates of treasury loans left in safekeeping by the school custodian and the policeman; security deposits for the rentals of stores; wedding rings waiting in pairs for the big day; various IOUs, the top one bearing the extravagant signature of the student, though it's easy to imagine that there are no funds to cover it; and finally, thick and thin bundles of government bonds. In a word, everything that was of value in the entire neighborhood, and to top it all, a satin-lined box containing a diamond necklace of unknown provenance. And now it's all gone with the wind. Interrogated on this subject, the masters would even have turned their pockets inside out as proof they had not taken a thing.

The apprentice with his bag of tools, a half-smoked cigarette in the corner of his mouth, sent precisely where there is strictly no unauthorized admission, will say nothing because he knows nothing. He pressed all the buttons in the crane as he was told to, in the correct sequence; when the impact came, all he did was blink. And look around in surprise, because he'd done exactly what his boss asked him to, nothing more and nothing less. In the cloud of dust that had instantly risen into the air, he could not have seen anything anyway. He merely wiped his watering eyes. And in that cloud of dust he himself also vanished. Even if someone had managed to take a photograph at the time, it would have recorded nothing but an impenetrable gray haze. The shock moved in a wave from the epicenter to the peripheries. The alleged accident shifted the layers of loose sand beneath the distant foundations. This circumstance, from one perspective most unpropitious, from another had many advantages. The more dramatic the events that the men in overalls managed to unleash, the more unquestioned would be the mass writing-off of every possible item from the inventories of one or another story. Having achieved their end, because once again they have succeeded, the masters and apprentices lock themselves in the storeroom and break out the bottles of untaxed spirit. Harmonica music accompanies them, plaintive and out of tune. They drink and sing, sing and weep. In the depths of their isolation, each of them separately becomes helpless. It is then that the greatest pain strikes them. They ask in a slurred voice why they are condemned to a life without women – them alone? In their despair they smash the empty bottles till the sound echoes away in the void into which they have been cast. Up on the heights they would at least have been something in the nature of angels with a golden touch. Yet what have they actually become, what? – they repeat, their furious gaze passing across the ceiling. One can only imagine the pandemonium they would create if on top of everything else they were given women. They'd probably suffer less, coming to terms with the shortcomings of their existence. The matter of their life without women is to remain closed for good. When they have emptied all the bottles, the balance sheet of their profits will be back at its point of departure. But business will continue to flourish, filling the same storeroom with new cases of bottles.

How agonizing it is to know about it all – about the illicit flow of goods, the mocking laughter in the back rooms – yet never to possess irrefutable proof. Helpless suspicions drift over the deserted marshaling yards like trembling balloons filled with hot air. In the meantime, deceitfulness oozes from every calculation, invoice, and specification list, and also from the bills that arrive in advance for urgent repairs not yet even commenced and paid for at twice the normal rate, for express service. There was no way to economize on repairs to the backdrops, since the plywood boards bearing the necessary painted images had been knocked down and smashed – they looked as if they had been through an earthquake. Indolent apprentices in overalls, suffering from the hiccups and convinced that nothing in this world was of any significance, were already at the warehouses pulling out other backdrops, whatever came to hand first. They were in a hurry and were not picking and choosing, since they had been instructed to act as quickly as possible to cover up the holes gaping on every side. It is the backdrops that determine the look of the world; they give it a trustworthy face and bolster faith in its substantiality, in the belief that everything the eye sees actually exists. There will be no other perspective than the one drawn on plywood boards at a deceptive angle, depicting the continuation of the street from the point where the wall and the pavement come to an end. Closing the space, the boards open it up at the same time, offering an illusory distance that seems to stretch into the unseen suburbs.

On the other side of the boards are all the hidden lighting installations and heating and cooling ducts; work is in full swing around the red-brick workshops, forklifts crisscrossing the whole time, though never cutting across the field of vision painted on the backdrops in the appropriate colors, with a predominance of yellow ochre imitating the hue of plasterwork. Thus, the workshops themselves are not seen either, nor the workmen in overalls, nor the huge gantry cranes, even though these are in constant use. Standing on the square as the first character at hand and gazing down the street, one is unable to imagine the real topography of the terrain. Besides, such surplus knowledge would be of no use to the characters. It's better to live tranquilly, though in the dark, and have no notion of what one is participating in. And if the order of things has already been disturbed, ignorance absolves one of inquiring into the reason, of wondering what led to the collapse. Whose calculations lay behind it, and which layers of sand were disturbed. Why those and not others. Here and there cracks had appeared; foundations had begun to settle dangerously, and a number of walls had collapsed on the spot. To avoid an unexpected and tragic end in one of the stories resembling this one, some hurried evacuations had to be arranged.

The apprentices fashion poles into a new construction to prop up the backdrop. They work quickly but unwillingly. After the last nail is knocked in, they move away at last to light up a longed-for cigarette. As chance would have it, the painted backdrops they took from the warehouses had been used once before in a story about the difficulties of life under an oppressive regime, and bore evident signs of censorship. To be precise, they were missing sizable fragments of pavement and wall, which had been removed along with the matching parts of the plywood base. It was not hard to guess why they had been cut out: to get rid of certain unsettling details that would have stirred recollections and emotions. It may have been, for example, that in this place there were bullet holes in a row, along with disturbing red smears. Repugnant circumstances, the memory of which some character harnessed to his own paltry drama of power had at one time attempted to erase, were written permanently into the background in this indirect way, through the removal of the traces they had left behind. Who reached for a saw to carry out such an order, when, and what did they get for it? Hardly anything, that much is certain. It was probably done by inexperienced apprentices, because only they – without the knowledge of the masters, and perhaps deceived by the trappings of majesty – could have violated the principle of paying no attention to the desires of the characters, and the practice of avoiding all contact with them. The largest holes were patched with pieces of thick cardboard, without even taking the trouble to color them ochre to conceal the repair. No eye will linger over them anyway. The gaze will rather be drawn towards the gaudy pennants jutting from the rows of windows painted on the plywood. This distant view was not without influence on the course of events; it reminded the concierges that in their apartment buildings too there were flags in the same national colors, stowed away in dusty closets and dark storage spaces beneath some flight of stairs or another, waiting for their time, which, so it seemed, had now come. Before long they flowered on the façades of the buildings round the square, restoring the equilibrium of bright accents between foreground and background. A wind blew up, opening the flags and setting them aflutter. This was the most emphatic sign that something had changed. The flags multiplied in windows; there were more and more of them by the minute. No one had known previously just how many had been lying about in various corners, but nor was anyone surprised. For of all the things one can think of, flags are the easiest to sew; no kind of faith or hope is required for the job.

And what about that other square, in a different story, of necessity vacated and closed down? And the suddenly interrupted threads of stories entwining it? And the inhabitants, removed from their own homes by a peremptory decree? Up till now they had lived where they belonged, uninitiated into the mysteries of the freight railroad, uninformed about the layers of sand shifting beneath the foundations of their houses or the economies made in the construction of the walls, far away from the notary and his safe. They did not know the overalled masters and they did not know whose account they were paying for; otherwise they never would have resigned themselves to the wrong they had suffered. Misfortune is easiest to accept when it is beyond comprehension. And now, unlike the notary, these people no longer had anything to worry about. The worst had already happened. In the place where they had lived till now, the ground had been pulled from under their feet.

So it should come as no surprise if they now begin to emerge from the streetcar at the stop in front of the local government offices. First just a handful of them – let's say one family, like a sign that is a prelude to the arrival of crowds. Someone has to take the first step, and this first step is from a later perspective nothing more than the presage of an already familiar continuation. Thus, the streetcar comes to a halt and the first refugees appear on the square: a small group of dark figures of different ages, in thick winter overcoats, caps with earflaps, head scarves, mufflers, and thick gloves. They tread unsurely, disoriented by the sudden downturn in their fortunes. The question of whether they may have come at the wrong time is the last thing they would wish to ask themselves. They too were not asked whether an explosion would be convenient for them. They hand down suitcases and bundles and arrange them on the sidewalk as if they believed – without so much as a hint of gratitude – that it had now been given over into their possession in return for the home they had lost. The streetcar cannot move on till they have finished unloading their belongings – till with the help of their children they have dragged out all the cardboard boxes tied with string, the sled, the teddy bear, the gramophone with its huge trumpet, and the canary in a cage. While they're maneuvering all these objects, they have something to do, and while there is something to do, there is also hope. Afterwards things will only get worse.

The moment the streetcar pulls away, they'll begin to look around helplessly, not knowing what to do with their luggage or themselves. They'll check whether they have brought the tureen with the gold band, a memento of the large service of best porcelain that they could not fit in their cases. They'll have a slight quarrel, allowing their raised voices to drift all the way up to the windows of the apartments. Then they'll press their ears to the trunks to check which one contains the ticking dining room clock. But ticking is nowhere to be heard, so they have to open the trunks and make sure that the clock is safely where they packed it, wrapped in a blanket. If it hadn't been for the haste imposed by unexpected events, they could have taken whole sets of tumblers and wine glasses, and they would have had time to wrap each individual one in tissue and pack it in sawdust. Yet if it hadn't been for those events beyond their control, why would they have left home in the first place? The youngest little girl is hugging a small pillow. It is her entire luggage. She stumbles as she carries her unwieldy burden, but she won't hear any word of encouragement, because the grown-ups have forgotten about the job they gave her. She's despondent and wants to return home. She was always the apple of their eye; so why is it that right now they don't hear her moaning and whimpering? She might be forgiven for thinking they have wads of invisible cotton wool stuck in their ears. When she stamps her little foot on the sidewalk, their gaze passes over her oblivious, wrapped in a mist of more important affairs. The pillow could just as well be lying on the curb, and that's where it falls. The little girl grabs at sleeves and coattails, to no avail. Since her desperation remains without a response, she begins to understand that there is no return to what was before, and that all her privileges are gone. She sits down on her pillow, her eyes wide open in astonishment. The tears that proved useless dry on her cheeks.

But the two older children still suspect nothing. While the policeman checks their parents' papers, they will feed the canary with a crust of bread stuck between the bars of the cage, abandoning their luggage unconcernedly on the sidewalk. The canary, tired from the journey, ruffles its feathers and turns its back on them. The only thing left is for them to run around in circles. And so they run till they're fit to drop, laughing wildly. Gleefully disobedient, for their own amusement they start running away from their mother and making faces from a distance at their father, who is walking round the square and, straining to be as polite as possible, which is understandable in his situation, is asking about a place to rent. The mother, in the meantime, is worn out. She sits on the suitcases, though she would rather have simply lain down on them. She is in an advanced state of pregnancy; her overcoat will not fasten across her belly, and she looks as if she could give birth at any moment. The children will keep hiding round the corner and coming back, hot and perspiring, until at the final moment, exhausted by their own giddiness, they burst into bitter tears. And it's plain to see that their laughter meant nothing, and that only their crying truly counts.

There is nothing to rent, nor could there be; each concierge sends the father on to the next building without so much as batting an eyelid. If only because of the cap with the earflaps and the thick winter coat, which smells of mothballs, drawing attention to itself and arousing mistrust. Otherness is always conspicuous from a distance, though it's hard to say how one recognizes it, if not from certain elusive attributes of cut and fabric. And what on earth kind of cut is that, what on earth sort of cloth is it, how can anyone wear something like that? – such questions automatically present themselves to the concierges, and especially to their wives. As for the upper windows overlooking the street, not many details can be seen from up there, but even so the first thing that will be noticed by the concerned occupants will be the foreignness of the handful of overcoats, incongruous as dark inkblots against the clean sidewalk, with its pattern of paving stones like squared office paper. Concerning the matter of foreignness, then, the locals need only a single glance, accustomed as they are to recognizing it in all its shades. There is no need for the mind to exert itself, and it's hard to be mistaken. The newcomers' attire does not blend subtly into the background; on the contrary, it is strikingly dark, and stands out in sharp contours displeasing to the eye. It can immediately be seen that they do not belong to this story. Foreignness, isolated within itself, is incapable of explaining itself, despite having introduced into the landscape a stain so disturbing it borders on deliberate provocation. Foreignness is foreign, and that is what constitutes its essence.

In the meantime, behind the lace curtains indignation is growing. If I am one of the respectable housewives following the doings of the newcomers from their windows, in my opinion the children ought to realize that they are not at home here. Because whether they feel at home determines what they are allowed to get away with. And if they do not understand this, the fault most certainly lies with their parents. The latter, however, are quite clearly occupied only with themselves and with what has happened to them somewhere else, and is of no concern to anyone here. Do people here not already have their own local worries? We have no need of new complications. And after all, it's quite possible that the newcomers, wrapped in their overcoats, scarves, and caps with earflaps, will bring with them a harsh climate foreign to this place: snowstorms or bitter frosts. One can only hope that if the threads of stories they have brought with them are immediately cut short, the newcomers will sit for a while on their suitcases and then, having nothing to latch on to, will disappear along with their luggage. They'll simply vanish into thin air, ending this unexpected breakdown of order, and the prior state of affairs will be happily restored. It's obvious, then, that they should not be given even the most cramped quarters to rent. Besides, for a paltry few pennies that may decrease in value anyway by tomorrow, no one will want to run the risk of problems such as icy drafts whistling through their apartment, especially since their entire supply of coal from the cellar would go up in smoke in the course of a few days. Why would they allow such a thing to happen when it's more than likely that the bad luck which has already driven these warmly dressed figures from their homes will continue to hold them in its grip?

Whatever one might think of the story taking place around the square, it was conceived as a light and smooth thing, and this fact bothered no one. It could have been told in a restrained tone of voice, without any trembling of the hands, without the need to touch on any weighty issues. Even if it contained a small amount of pain, this pain was shot through with comicality. And if a policeman appeared in it, it was only because of his amusing qualities – in other words, so he could strut about in his ill-fitting uniform. The handsome student was needed for balance, so the maid should also have someone to be sweet on. Everything was fashioned to a middling size, so there was no danger of choking on one's laughter, nor of shedding a single tear. The suffering in the story did not assume the kinds of dimensions that would exhaust one's reserves of sympathy, giving a lie to the belief that these are unlimited. Did it bother anyone that the notary pinches the maid, that the maid has a crush on the student, or that the policeman has eyes for the maid? What of it that the notary's tired, overweight body refuses to obey him, or that the student is shown in a less than complimentary light by the professors' comments in his grade book and by the excesses of behavior in which he has distinguished himself? What of it that the policeman, worn down by constantly being passed over for promotion, no longer has a heart for his duties and contents himself with an outward show of conscientiousness? No one minded about the cream cakes in the glass display case, even if one or another of them turned out to be inedible. There were no complaints.

It would be best for the newcomers to go away again, allowing the continuation of a story to which they did not belong. But it seems instead that because of them, all local matters will have to take a new turn. For when the streetcar stops again outside the government offices, more and more new arrivals start climbing down in an endless stream, struggling with unwieldy packages and tugging teary-eyed children behind them. And since it had fallen to their lot to leave so abruptly, and they did not know if they would ever return, they had to put on their winter overclothes. If they had been asked about the smell of mothballs, they would have said they hadn't had time to air their things.

The windows of the local government offices would offer the best view of the scene below, with its ever-increasing numbers of dark padded overcoats and the accompanying bundles, trunks, and suitcases. The first few dark specks against the background of the sidewalk rapidly spread into a large ink stain. Looking down from above, one could see how many of the new arrivals were already encamped on the square and how many were still emerging from the streetcar. A trembling old woman is having trouble negotiating the step, but she has no need of anyone's assistance since a first grader in pigtails is with her and will help her down. Alas, there is no bench for the grandmother to sit on, though that is all she wants. A blind man in dark glasses taps at the step with his white cane before cautiously placing his foot on it. With one hand always occupied, he was able to take with him only a single small piece of luggage, which is actually just a violin case, and it would be hard to say what he packed in it – food, a change of underwear, or an instrument. Following the blind man, a flock of children pours out of the streetcar, black mourning bands on their arms. They jostle one another noisily. They're from an orphanage, which evidently also collapsed. The black is fresh in some cases; other armbands have faded. Each was probably sewn at some time in an impulse of the heart by a compassionate aunt shaken by the sudden misfortune in the family. She would have liked to be of more service, but she lacked the strength, and since she was unable to take the orphan in, she merely attached the child's mourning to his sleeve with black tacking, and so it remained.

The discolored black moves no one; it becomes commonplace when seen on every second arm. The inhabitants of the apartment buildings have paused in their gateways and are staring at those who no longer have a home. It may be that as they do so they feel something in the manner of sympathy, but if I am one of these observers moved by their own goodness, after a moment I have to turn away in embarrassment. Sympathy that is utterly devoid of readiness to help seems to me discomfiting and unnecessary. It'll occur to me rather that our hearts are too soft, that's the problem. Besides, is pity not pathetic in itself?

Who is the pity for? For an overabundant multitude in which each figure bears some mark of unsightliness corresponding to imperfections in their clothing. The idea that these blemishes conceal faults of character suggests itself automatically. The first impression is unfavorable. They are too big or too small, too skinny or too fat. The more of these figures there are, the more clearly the ugliness can be seen to be distributed among them in equal measure.

Multiplied by a sufficiently large number, the defects of appearance encumber the entire crowd like collective guilt. And the newcomers are as numerous as the inhabitants of the square; the latter will feel overwhelmed and powerless in the face of the distressing change that the mild morning has brought them without any warning. They begin to fill with resentment, because they see that above all they themselves are the victims. The change has been imposed at the cost of space that is rightfully theirs. To say nothing of the fact that their flower bed, the centerpiece of the square, has no hope of surviving intact. But to the painful question of why the refugees are encamped under their windows in particular, there will be no reply. If this is my story, I observe the development of events with distaste and resignation. It wasn't the purpose of the streetcar to bring this wretched crowd. And now what has happened has happened, and cannot be changed.

The sheer numbers of this uninvited mass would have appalled the clerks of the government offices if they had not previously abandoned their observation posts by the windows overlooking the square. They would have watched the green of the lawn disappear entirely from view, everything blocked out by the overcoats – a profusion of dark cloth, black and navy blue, beneath which was the unseen padding, and beneath that the smooth lining. Nor was that all: beneath the lining there were successive layers of fabric, all the way down to fustian undergarments. The material made of different kinds of fibers disturbs the purity of the space – it's crammed together tightly in its excess, which accompanies the excess of characters. Under cover of an opaque curtain of mixed shades and textures, the newcomers may well end up trampling the flower bed. Looking down on the square at the present moment, the clerks, and especially their bosses, would have had to ask the official questions: who are these people, where are they from, and what ought to be done with them? Should they be dispatched without delay back where they came from, or, on the contrary, should a room be set up in the offices where they can turn in their applications and be issued residence permits bearing treasury stamps and a seal with the national emblem? But there is no one left to wonder what should be done with the crowd, which has gradually taken over the entire expanse of the square and is now sitting about on suitcases amid the lingering smell of mothballs, waiting for who knows what conclusion.

An order announced by megaphone has settled the matter

of pedestrian traffic: from now on nonresidents are prohibited from crossing the boundary line of the streetcar tracks. What more could be demanded of the policeman in the face of so many adverse circumstances, which his absent superiors have left him to deal with on his own? It will not be at all easy to immortalize them in his daily report. He's already done everything within his power. He did not forget to check the identification documents of the newcomers, or even to prepare a short memo, at least concerning the first family that arrived, before his pencil broke. Did he not ask searching questions about the children from the orphanage? He even managed to establish that before they were brought here on the streetcar they had been left to their own devices by their irresponsible or perhaps helpless guardians. If I am the policeman, no coup d'état will release me from duties that have become onerous to me, nor will it relieve me of the nuisance of having to submit reports. Nor do I know, or want to know, about the destruction that cannot be seen from here, unless my superiors inform me about it in a separate memorandum setting out exactly what is expected of me. Considering his meager salary, the policeman still manages to maintain an exemplary orderliness on his beat, while everywhere around him promotions are being handed out to arrogant striplings with no experience and no accomplishments, people whose only strong point turns out to be their handwriting. Nor will things be different this time; the policeman will be kept from advancement by superiors with the same taste for calligraphy as their predecessors, whose star has just fallen and been extinguished.

This is where the painful heart of the matter lies: in poorly formed letters and spelling mistakes. In the inflexible yet obscure principles of grammar. Thoughts flounder unhappily among them, straightforward yet entangled. There exists an exception to every rule, and so no rule can be relied upon. Every evening, with the same chewed-up pen in his hand, the policeman laboriously composes his clumsy sentences; the nib creaks torpidly, and ink spatters on the sheet of foolscap. It's all for nothing. His only reward is scorn and disregard, and perpetual injustice done to him and his family. After all these years of service there has been no raise, even though he has a wife and children to support. His uniform allowance goes towards the costs of daily life, and even so he's barely able to make ends meet. On top of everything, he even has to pay for the ink out of his own pocket. Since this is how things are, the policeman with his rather watery gaze cannot be expected to see through the falsifications in the invoices circulating far beyond his reach, nor to notice the actions of the true perpetrators of the confusion, since there has not even been a notification from which he could have learned about the existence of the back areas. How then could he have perceived the connection between it and the catastrophe brought about deliberately so as to kick over the traces? All the more, then, the policeman cannot be expected of his own volition to gather evidence in a matter for which the arms of even the highest-ranking functionaries are not long enough, and their eyes too slow; or that he alone will set the bureaucratic machine in motion. He would have to be mad to exert himself to such extremes.

By midday there was not a single wedding picture left in the window of the photographer's studio. The portrait of the movie actress in the white fur coat had also disappeared, and in its place there was a brand-new display: a greatly enlarged and therefore blurred picture of a man with a row of medals on his snow white marshal's uniform. Instead of a lingering glance from beneath long lashes there was a piercing, supercilious gaze that penetrated the viewer like a bullet from a shotgun. When it was already clear that the political upheaval had turned into a dictatorship, this photograph was put on special show, as if a new kind of service were being offered. The owners of the local stores, which had been emptied of goods, felt obliged to order a copy. One could also buy the picture already mounted. In this way, properly framed, it was seen in every shopwindow round the square, without exception, in every case draped with ribbons in the national colors decorated with artificial posies, and propped up behind with brown glass bottles. If a fly were accidentally to have fallen into one of those bottles it would have remained there, drowned in the remains of stale beer. Amid static and white noise, radio sets kept announcing a speech that would be broadcast soon, at twelve o'clock precisely. Even those who had no radio understood that they were not to miss this address. Before the intently awaited voice was heard, for some time the sky was crisscrossed by the trajectories of sharp glances from beneath the military cap that had been duplicated ahead of time in the photographer's darkroom. They intersected above the square, above the streetcar, above the crowd in their warm overcoats huddled together on suitcases and listlessly chewing their last remaining food. In the meantime, one concierge after another stopped the policeman and complained that the refugees were continually disobeying the ordinance, crossing the iron ring of the tracks, and furthermore with bad intentions, namely, to pee in a gateway. So with a heavy sigh, for he had had enough, the policeman finally ordered the faucet in the middle of the square to be turned off – if the newcomers don't drink water then at least they won't need to pee.

Bit by bit, for the moment only outside the streetcar tracks, what the concierges called order began to be restored. But true order was still a long way off. For example, no one gave a thought to the abandoned government offices. Since there were no clerks at the desks, someone else had to take matters into their own hands. A handful of grammar school boys, rounded up on the way by the student, dragged the radio set in its heavy casing from his tiny room in the attic. They set it up on a tall stepladder and turned the volume up to the maximum. The refugees confined within the circle of the streetcar tracks had nowhere to hide from the chaotic stream of hisses and crackles that immediately poured from the loudspeaker. On this very stream, a moment later there flowed the anticipated speech, foaming with rhetorical questions and filled with meaningful pauses and exclamations fired in salvos. The grammar school custodian, who had lent the boys the ladder and an extension cord, was not in the habit of judging the rightfulness of truths proclaimed over his head, which always drop on their victims from on high, as ruthless as the winged predators with hooked talons that appear on the national emblem. He allowed the speech to pass him by in its entirety, an approving yet distracted look on his face. But he did not stint in his praise for the radio set, and repeated to anyone who came along that in comparison with that miracle of technology any other radio was nothing. Lastly, to the powers that had just fallen he addressed a question tinged with irritation and marked by a slight nasal tone, like all grievances – to wit, why had there been no speeches and no amplification of this kind before?

In the meantime the crowd was swarming round the flower bed, straining within the boundaries to which it had been confined, and too numerous to be able to follow all the orders and prohibitions: every few minutes one or another group, borne on a wave, suddenly and against their own will found themselves beyond the cordon, like castaways. Driven back by the fists and boots of the concierges, they had to summon their last reserves of strength to swim against the current and submerge themselves anew in the throng crammed within the line of the tracks. The limits imposed on the newcomers were the official price for their unacceptable presence, and expressed the silent demand that they do their best to disappear without delay. This, however, was beyond their capabilities: the body has its substance, which even with the best will in the world is not able to melt into thin air from one moment to the next. Lacking sofas, armchairs, bedrooms, and dining rooms, each refugee could not have occupied less space, but even that was too much. As for the local people, in the policeman's view they would have been well advised under the present circumstances to stay at home. But if they refused, nothing could be done about it. Listed residents who paid their rent and their taxes had certain rights. So it was hard to put an end to the barter that had been the start of all the ebbings and flowings the crowd was barely able to cope with around its edges. In the rapid transactions a beautiful past was readily exchanged for the illusion of relief, which comes at once but does not last long. On the other hand, in order to acquire someone else's past for a song, one had only to go to one's reserves and give so little of them that there was no question it was worth it, and so nobody hesitated for long.

Before the speech came to an end, the tureen with the gold band had been traded for a loaf of stale bread. The newcomers agreed to this price quickly and compliantly, as if they had been hungry for many days, whereas in reality – if one can speak here at all of reality – only a few hours earlier they had still been eating breakfast in their own home. Yet it was unimaginably far away, in another story, and the table from which they had eventually had to get up no longer even existed now. It had vanished along with the empty shells in the eggcups, along with the coffee-pot and the butter dish. The bread crusts had survived: the children, making faces, had thrust them in their pockets when their mother wasn't looking. But the crusts too had already been eaten, and now the children were complaining they were hungry. So it was unclear how the hours should be counted, since even the dining room clock, despite having been wrapped carefully in tablecloths and placed in the trunk, had ceased ticking. The unexpected severing of the threads of the story they had inhab-ited had changed all sorts of things. From that moment conti-nuity in their lives was lost, the more so because time had proved to be relative while space had suddenly collapsed. What sort of journey was it of which it could be said only that it had a begin-ning and an end? A beginning in a luggage-filled hallway, an end at a streetcar stop, and in between nothing, nothing whatsoever, just the void that extends between one story and another. A closer look at the overcoats, for instance, would reveal that they were of no worse quality than the local light autumn coats. Not conforming to the requirements of local custom, the overcoats had remained in accord with the background that had now van-ished, and that they went with much better. But without a natu-ral backdrop, they were no match for local fashions, which were self-assured because they belonged here, and were unshakable as anything self-evident always is. The newcomers' overcoats were pointed at in scorn because of their overbroad cut, excessively padded shoulders and too-wide collars, details that on foreign ground could not be defended from mockery. In fact they were also old-fashioned, though only insofar as the reality they had previously been immersed in had permanently gone out of style. Beneath many of the collars torn in a tussle with some concierge there still lingered the scent of good-quality cologne. Traces of wear and tear appeared on them at an accelerated rate; hence the cuffs, for instance, which in normal circumstances are the first things to grow threadbare, were in excellent condition, and where a button had gone missing at the neck, freshly snapped threads could be seen.

Just like the space, the sequence of events here bears the marks of a drastic shortcut. And as usual in such circumstances, it's a question of money. It was out of economy that the shortened perspectives of space and time arose. The cost of the whole enterprise is enormous even without the refugees, and the profit negligible. The losses that have been sustained thus far because of botched work, fraud, and deliberate sabotage – unbelievably brazen abuses carried out with absolute impunity – encourage the curtailing of expenses, though the latter will always end up being too high. Space is not cheap, but time costs the most. The more lazily it flows, channeling out its meanders, slowly revealing multiple strata beneath the ground and permitting events to gradually mature, the higher will be the final bills for sunlight. The refugees are refugees; their fate is sealed and is plain to see for everyone but themselves – there is no place for them, neither here nor back there. In this matter a miracle is the most they can count on. Then would it not be better if all that is ordained for them were to happen at once? Such is the inevitable conclusion of dry calculations which cannot be doubted and which also, in the final reckoning, can serve the interests of the refugees themselves, by sparing them hours of suffering.

Time works to the advantage of the local people, though without their being able to claim any credit for the fact. They can pick and choose, rooting around in open suitcases, haggling, then paying. They lug home cheaply acquired still-lifes in heavy frames, table lamps with shades and a canary in a cage. The handles of plated silverware jut from their pockets. Feverishly animated, yet with absolute self-possession, they were fully aware that the appearance of other people's property on the square was a unique opportunity – the best bargain of their entire life lay within arm's reach. The more laughable foreignness became as it manifested itself in the cut of overcoats, the more it excited and attracted in the gleam of metal, in high-quality wood and immaculate porcelain. In light of the empty shelves in local stores, every carton of cheap cigarettes from someone's emergency reserves was worth a silver cigarette case. Anyone who wanted could even have bought a gold medal for bravery and pinned it on their autumn coat.

It was right there in the middle of the square that the school custodian, appointed messenger, went looking for the missing clerks. The latter, however, felt no sense of obligation, having learned from the radio that the government had been ousted. In the endless buzzing and crackling that had preceded the communiqué, the wily senior civil servants had recognized an approaching time of confusion. They foresaw that from now on until further notice, inactivity would be rewarded, while any manifestation of conscientiousness could meet with chance retribution. When the custodian found them, they shrugged and quickly slipped away into the crowd. Only two of the junior clerks obeyed the summons with a naïve readiness. Embarrassed by the circumstances in which they had been caught unawares, one with a crocheted napkin in his hand, the other carrying a box of lead soldiers, they straightened their jackets and their crooked neckties and let themselves be led to where new duties were supposedly awaiting them. Yet this does not mean at all that they returned to their offices and their hard chairs at desks by the windows overlooking the flower bed. Following the custodian, they calmly passed the gateway with the damaged emblem and continued on to the café at number one. The waiter had not received any instructions from the proprietor, so the café was closed and at the same time open: open for some and closed for others, its blinds half down. At an agreed-upon signal – the custodian rapped on the windowpane, rat-a-tat-tat – the key in the lock on the inside turned with a creak.

Before the two clerks gave the waiter their hats, the student stood from his table and greeted them; he had known both of them for a long time, having been, let's say, at school with them.

One of the clerks had, for example, a brother-in-law in the fraternity, while another was impressed by the metal insignia on the student's lapel. Only fifteen minutes earlier the latter had pushed his pant legs into tall boots and buckled a military-style leather belt round his jacket, which instantly destroyed the charm of his shapely and well-made civilian attire, but on the other hand gave his clothing an air of insolent arrogance that would not stop at anything. Before the student decided how tight to fasten the belt, in his attic he had spent a long time staring at himself in the shaving mirror, an operation that required complicated maneuvers, including many turns to the left and right as if he were on parade, so that from the fragments of reflections he could finally obtain some notion of the whole. The clerks had to agree that he deserved all the official and private assistance he could get, given the duties he had taken upon himself in the present situation. He smiled to himself at the very thought of how much now depended upon him. He dismissed the custodian right away – he was to go back to his post. The waiter danced around him, exercising his profession to the full, anticipating the other man's wishes. Before the clerks appeared, the student had managed to knock back a glass of sweet liqueur; they drank one more glass together as a toast to the new order, all on the house.

They immediately faced many more tasks than glasses; flipping through the notes he had hurriedly penciled on rustling paper napkins, the student listed a significant number of jobs that needed doing, and it goes without saying that these were not inconsequential personal matters but quite the opposite, public affairs of great weight. The most urgent of them seemed to be the establishment of a volunteer guard for maintaining law and order. Its core was to be constituted by a handful of grammar school pupils waiting obediently by the cloakroom. They were the same ones who had earlier helped to set up the amplification for the radio address. The undertaking had not been especially successful, though the crowd gathered on the square had been too busy with other matters to notice. Before the speech came to an end, the loudspeaker gave a wheeze, burned out, and fell silent. This was its response to dangerous modifications being carried out by one of the boys. Let's say it was the smart aleck in round glasses who had quickly turned the radio up and converted it by adding a megaphone. Though it ended up being destroyed, he was still proud of what he had achieved. The smart aleck in round glasses is the notary's son, whose mother is waiting for him so impatiently. He's in no hurry to go home. He did an honest job to deserve the prize awarded to him and his pals: the special privilege of standing sentry, that is to say the assignment of admitting volunteers, one after another, into the recruitment office set up inside the grammar school.

It's entirely possible that it was actually situated in the biology lab, among rows of dusty jars containing specimens in formaldehyde. Many things could be seen there that would later give one nightmares: a horse's stomach in cross section, no longer capable of digestion; the innocent heart of the horse; its cloudy, tormented eye. But the commission to which the commander of the newly formed unit appointed the two junior clerks did not even look in that direction. They handed around cigarettes and lit up from one another like brothers in arms in the trenches. They scattered ash everywhere and told each other vulgar stories as a sign that now everything had changed, and that they themselves already knew this and had nothing against it. Quite the opposite, they liked the new state of affairs much better than the old one. The more uncertainty they felt, the louder the choruses of laughter exploded over and again. But whenever any one of them glanced out the window, he recovered his faith in the purpose and meaning of the whole enterprise, because volunteers were gathering outside the gate, already in uniform, wearing the same grammar school overcoats they wore every day, with the twin rows of metal buttons. They had learned from one another about the recruitment; each of them clutched in his sweaty hands an application written on a torn-out page from an exercise book. Many still had their school satchels on, though they were embarrassed by this, sensing that the contents were too incriminating. Especially the notebooks with correspondence between their teachers and their parents: these diminished not only their own dignity but also that of the selection commission and the honorable service they were seeking to enter. At the sound of a handbell lent to the commission by the custodian, they came and went without asking any questions.

Since there were more than enough candidates, the clerks did little more than skim through their scribbled applications, which all ended in a request that the undersigned be accepted; they slid the letters casually to one another across the tabletop, amid the ashtrays, while the commander dozed in his seat for a short while after his sleepless night, a thin ribbon of saliva dripping from the corner of his mouth. The contents of the application were of no significance. They took only the older-looking boys who were already starting to sprout mustaches, sending the smaller ones home and making an exception only for a handful of special cases who, for their contribution to the operation involving the loudspeaker on the square, had already been issued with armbands as order guards – these were white and bore the round stamp of their office, thus raising them in importance over all the rest. Among these individuals, however, one more exception was made, for the son of the notary. In the presence of everyone he was forced to remove the official stamped armband from his sleeve, after which he was dismissed without a word of explanation, even though he too had made his contribution, and was by no means one of the smallest. Convinced that there had been a mistake, almost in tears, he afterwards hammered on the door of the biology lab. He was still making a fuss when the commission locked themselves in the room and began to tidy their papers. Finally, at a command tossed over someone's shoulder, his pals who had been accepted into the guard grabbed him by the arms, frog-marched him down the stairs, and threw him out the gate.

Where he got to after that is hard to say. For obvious reasons he was unable to go very far. His family had heard something, perhaps from the concierge, who had seen him and his friends lifting the loudspeaker onto the stepladder, or maybe from the policeman, who had learned firsthand about the recruitment for the order guard. They sent the maid to the school – the boy's mother demanded his immediate return home. The school custodian blocked the maid's way and asked her for the password, which naturally she did not know. So he refused to allow her up the stairs until she reluctantly answered certain indiscreet questions that occurred to him in an imaginative moment, and until on top of that he had pinched her plump backside. He didn't accompany her upstairs, as he had been on duty ever since he'd taken upon himself the duties of a watchman. On the other side of the lab door a hum of male voices could be heard. Before knocking, she peeped through the keyhole. But she could see nothing except billows of white cigarette smoke. The moment she opened the door and stood on the threshold, however, she was greeted with a burst of laughter. She thought they were laughing at her. Straight in front of her she saw the specimens in their jars. Her heart and her stomach were probably contracting even without this additional sight. Her gaze immediately encountered the disquieting stare of the horse's eye. If I am the maid, as I peer through the white haze the last thing I would expect is to spot a familiar steel gray sweater on the other side of the table.

In such a case there was nothing to be done but drop one's eyes and stare at the floor. The laughter died down, but they did not offer her a chair. Let her stand where the recruits had stood before, in front of the commission sprawling in their chairs at the table. No one says anything, and it's obvious to the maid that they are waiting to see what he will say – the handsomest and most important one among them. The student holds back for a long time. Instead of speaking, he rings the bell. He looks at the notary's maid, right at her, but his gaze is cold. If I am her, it's my turn now. Even if my legs collapse beneath me, I have to state the business I was sent on: that the boy inherited poor health from his father. Here I will throw into the balance the long name of the hereditary illness he suffers from. Let the majesty of medical science force the respect for the family's wishes that the lady of the house expects. Yet the name of the illness has completely vanished from her memory. The student smokes, his elbows propped on the tabletop, while she stammers, by now counting only on his compassion. But he has no compassion for her. And even if on a whim he decided to help her, he could do no more than point through the window at his unit of recruits doing push-ups in the school yard.

He gazed at his men in silence, for a moment forgetting anything else. Did they not look superb – tough and utterly obedient? She was supposed to point out which one it was. From a distance they all looked alike. Nevertheless, after a short moment she was certain he was not among them. Though she was frightened and in despair, still she could not conceal her admiration when she looked at him, and he could not fail to see it. If I am the commander, this chubby mare with fat fetlocks isn't exactly my type. She hides her timid gaze under half-closed eyelids and keeps blushing, and on top of everything else there's that unfashionable calico frock. From the screen in the dark movie theater he had known many women. None of them had a stutter. All carried themselves stylishly. He rang the bell again: her business bored him, and he'd had enough. Nevertheless, he followed her out into the hallway. For a moment he looked down onto the square, flicking ash on the windowsill. He watched her walk alongside the streetcar tracks, slowly, like a beast of burden loaded beyond measure. She could obviously bear a great deal. In fact, he had noticed this at once. He peered down to see where she disappeared from sight: she entered the gateway of number seven, as he suspected. The commander lost himself in thought, gazing into the depths of the entrance-way, till he was brought back to reality by the sight of the notary leaving the place. As commander of the order guard, he had to admit that the best thing the notary could do at this point was to begin searching for his son of his own accord without relying on other people.

In the meantime, the crowd encamped in the square was

growing more and more exhausted. Rumors were starting to circulate about taxicabs that at a cost would take anyone who wanted to a better place. That better place was supposedly America. Word spread in the blink of an eye. With renewed hope, though not without a struggle, the refugees tried to imagine America, with its lofty mansions, its sleek skyscrapers, its metal needles thrusting upward in profusion. Many of the refugees, not knowing what still awaited them and what opportunities would present themselves, had already sold their more valuable possessions, and were now beginning to regret their hasty transactions, for how would they be able to make a home in America without their belongings? They could no longer digest the mouthfuls of dark bread they had swallowed. For the truth is that hunger can be tolerated so long as there is hope, and it is not advisable to give in to doubt too readily. Others regretted the missed opportunity to get rid of part of their luggage, which would not fit into any automobile. Resignation would develop slowly in minds and hearts like an insidious disease, reaching its final, overt stage no sooner than when it was already evident no taxicabs would be arriving from the side streets, where the pavement ended just beyond the corner; nor, even more obviously, would any leave from here. Looking for them in the distance was useless. The fact that the rumors about America were dreamed up out of nothing was obvious to the locals from the start. They simply shrugged, because they happened to know that there is no America. They counted rather on local means, on orderliness being restored by their own efforts – in brief, on the order guard, which embarked on its duties without delay.

Even if the memory of a good life in peaceful times was still fresh in the minds of the refugees, that life was over, and now others were making the decisions in matters that concerned them, driving them from place to place, with their luggage or, if need be, without. But when the luggage was finally gathered in one place, and the refugees in another, and it seemed certain that in just another moment the worst chaos would be under control, and order reinstated – suddenly, out of nowhere, the streetcar returned, crammed with new refugees exhausted from the crush, half-suffocated, barely alive. There were newlyweds fresh from their wedding, the confetti still in their hair, he in black, she in white; the smiles had not yet entirely faded from their lips, yet in their eyes there was already consternation. So they held one another firmly by the hand, just in case circumstance conspired to separate them. There was a woman with a large bouquet of roses in her arms; the flowers were still striking, though they had gotten a little squashed. The bouquet is heavy, so as if out of habit she looks round for someone who up till now she could always hand them over to – perhaps a chauffeur. But here there is no chauffeur and no automobile. No one knows how she ended up in the streetcar, nor who pushed her in there. Her white fur stands out conspicuously against the background of dark overcoats; if someone had been waiting for her, they would have spotted her at once.

But no one is waiting and no one even stares at her, neither the members of the order guard nor the policeman. She's already hidden behind other new arrivals – thin ones, fat ones, each less attractive than the last. What about her, the beautiful woman in the fur? Perhaps she too would eventually reveal some defect of appearance? Yes, indeed. Puffy eyes, a tear-streaked face, and running mascara. No doubt she would wish to call her agent and have him extricate her from all this without delay. But where is there a telephone? Perhaps in the café across the way? The guards block her path: she is not allowed to cross over there, and besides, the café is closed. Since this is the case, the woman in the fur coat mentions the notary, giving his name and address. Winking at one another, they promise to inform the notary of her presence. It's not hard to predict that they will do nothing for her whatsoever, yet she expects help, since it is beyond her comprehension that her voice and her looks could have lost their charm. Even if they were well-intentioned, the two guards would do no more than ask the policeman for his opinion. If they were not afraid to bother him with trivial matters. Because from the very beginning the policeman made a show of ignoring the order guard. He was immune to the lofty atmosphere surrounding it. He avoided the guardsmen; he was not interested in collaborating with them, and instead of carrying out the commander's instructions he preferred to give orders himself, though even that he did reluctantly. Left to rely on their own judgment, the guards knew only that the crowd was not allowed to spread out. One exception would immediately lead to another. They had this principle from their commander in his tall boots, and lacking anything else they could cling to, whether experience or their own opinions, they had to follow it blindly.

It was hard to maintain order with nothing but one's raised voice and bare hands. Several of them had grown hoarse at once. A directive was issued announcing the confiscation of all walking sticks, and sure enough all canes, including the white one, were deposited in the place indicated; subsequently, in the hands of the guards the canes became an instrument for control. These batons were almost as good as the one lost in the early morning by the commander, which had been exhaustively searched for but not found. In the situation the guards found themselves in, it was necessary time and again to swing their cane at someone, to give themselves confidence, which is never in sufficient supply. Looking around for their leader, the guardsmen suddenly noticed they were alone. The commander had vanished at some unknown moment, for some unknown purpose. He had disappeared without a word to anyone, and they could only hope that he was not far away, given how little space there was anyway. His subordinates could see that now orderliness depended entirely on their diligence – that is to say, the blows of their batons – and so things will remain, let's say, for the next half an hour. Till the commander, intoxicated with power and success, will come running down the kitchen steps of the building at the back of the courtyard at number seven, hurriedly fastening the military belt over his jacket.

No one knew when the airmen had woken up in the hotel. Their job involved inspecting air force bases, and after particularly enjoyable banquets they would sometimes wake in completely unknown places. Wrenched from sleep, for a while they had stared in stupefaction at the anonymous walls of the hotel room papered in a striped pattern that meant nothing to them. For a long time they twisted and turned in bed in their crumpled undergarments, trying to recall how they came to be here, but their memory had retained only the round zero on the roof of the streetcar they had stepped down from at dawn. So they cocked their ears and listened intently, not understanding a thing. They looked out the window and could not believe what they saw. Afterwards, they had probably shaved in the utmost haste, cursing as they nicked their skin and passing one another a stick of alum. Astonished that there was no one to order breakfast from, they drank what was left of the coffee in their own thermos flasks, and by a side table near the deserted reception desk they thumbed briefly through old newspapers whose rustling explained little to them. The adjutant's portable shortwave radio refused to work; from that moment it remained utterly silent even when the general attempted to tune it. They found the front door locked shut. The staff had evidently fled to their homes. In order to leave, the airmen had to combine forces to break down the door.

Soon afterwards they turned up in the local government offices, in uniforms buttoned up tight. They passed through a series of empty rooms till they reached the office of the director on the highest floor. The window there had opened of its own accord, and the lace curtain was fluttering outside like a white flag hung out as a sign of surrender. It could also be seen from the square, alone amid so many other flags dazzling the eyes with the bright national colors. A gust of wind had blown some documents off the desk and onto the floor. The officers stepped on them unceremoniously, as though they were wastepaper; they stood around the black telephone and took turns shouting into the receiver, trying to reach the headquarters of an airfield that only they knew. Amid the dry crackling on the line, they finally heard a distant, barely audible voice that promised to send a helicopter for them. It would come after lunch, they repeated to one another, not worrying for a minute about whether it would find the place. It was questionable whether they had properly understood everything, and whether the promise made by the unknown speaker would be kept. It was enough to look out the window at the sky to realize that meteorological conditions were unfavorable. The helicopter would have to make its way through a vast covering of snow clouds, a dense and unbroken mass whose dirty white coloring would have prevented the pilot from seeing not just the network of geographic coordinates, but also the sequence of dates on the calendar.

The airmen settled themselves in armchairs and on sofas. They began to wait for who knows what, dislodged from the routine of their daily affairs and just as lost as the refugees on the square below. They yawned, stretched, brushed the office dust off their uniforms. They killed time in accordance with their rank: the general drummed his fingers on the desktop; the major whistled as he paced from wall to wall, his hands thrust into his pockets; the captain took out some marbles, and the lieutenant began making paper airplanes out of official documents and launching them from the open window, till his fingers got caught in the window frame, at which point he cursed and quit what he was doing. In spite of everything the airmen were better off than the refugees, if only because they were not dressed in dark padded overcoats, like the crumpled rank and file of the distant catastrophe, but on the contrary in well-made officers' uniforms at the sight of which, at dawn that day, the policeman's hand had of its own accord snapped to the shining peak of his cap. Elegance engendered respect. In a natural manner it guaranteed lightness and unlimited freedom for the airmen's bodies, which consequently were, as always, prepared to rise effortlessly into space, let alone walk up an ordinary staircase to some floor of a local government building. The destiny of the accursed padded overcoats, on the other hand, was to descend from the steps of the streetcar ever lower, and to settle amid the smell of mothballs, which also drifted close to the ground, being heavier than clean air, while the closed circle of the tracks marked their implacable boundary. The overcoats had rapidly turned into a bedraggled, shapeless, padded sign of foreignness, a ballast that weighed on the shoulders only so that the crowd of new arrivals should once and for all sink to the cobbled floor of the square, as if they had drowned.

Enjoying rare privileges, the airmen seemed nevertheless not to notice them or to appreciate them – for them and for many others, these privileges were unquestionable and only too well deserved. But it was precisely for the uniforms that room was found in the soft armchairs – not for the bodies, which were able to relish comfort only when the opportunity presented itself, though they were filled with their own characteristic pride and an illusory belief that the world lay at their feet. In reality it lay at the legs of their uniform pants, and at their polished regulation boots. What would the general's protruding belly, or the adjutant's skinny ribs, have been without the insignia of rank? No sign, no indication that could have guided fate, was written on their delicate pink skin. Any integument seems an equally suitable costume in the face of sudden death or lucky survival, in scenes of adulation or abasement. The body has no influence and thus is of scant significance. And since this is the case, despite the neatly trimmed mustache, despite the cool glint of confidence in the eye, despite the bold gestures and the courteous loftiness coloring every utterance in a natural manner before it leaves the lips, bodies alone are at home in any situation. They belong just as well in comfortable armchairs or at a large desk with phone at hand as they do on the bare pavement down there below, where there is no access to a telephone even in matters of the utmost urgency. What, therefore, could give a body importance and define its capabilities, if not that most important circumstance: the quality of the fabric and the cut of the garment?

The image of the refugees emerging from the streetcar in their dark overcoats, victims of an unknown disaster who from a sudden twist of narrative lost not just the roof over their heads but also the freedom to regulate their own affairs and due respect – this image, then, from the very beginning called for an appropriate counterbalance. And so the presence of a few fine-looking officers seemed to all those witnessing the events, especially the defenders of local law and order, to be no accident – rather, it was a historical necessity that in its own way was obvious and well-grounded in realities familiar to everyone, against the background of the yellowing plaster. And since the officers were seen entering the government building in their immaculate uniforms, no one doubted that they knew best what needed to be done next.

Thus, by virtue of his rank and the braiding he wore, the air force general was obliged to receive a report from the commander of the order guard. He even clapped him on the shoulder, offered him a cigarette with a classy mouthpiece, and attempted discreetly to find out what on earth was going on here, since from the very beginning he'd been unable to make head or tail of it: in his story, from which he had come and to which he intended to return, the best military order prevailed, and he was unaccustomed to anything else. He was willingly given exhaustive explanations, from which he understood even less. The guards, who were lined up two deep in the hallway, at an order from their commander raised an appropriate cheer, upon which a dust-covered picture fell off the wall. And since he was expected to, the general personally gave the at-ease. He could have demanded much more – the soldiers would eagerly have obeyed any instruction whatever that was lit up by the golden sheen of the braid on his collar. But he did not deign to issue any other orders.

The column of guards had barely marched away, their boots clattering on the stairs, when a line of petitioners formed outside the director's office. For instance, the baker in his white apron was prepared to bake rolls for the refugees right away, so long as he received an official guarantee that his costs would be reimbursed. He presented one part of his calculations then and there, writing columns of figures on a sheet of paper; the other part he would not share with anyone, keeping it to himself as a trade secret. What had happened was that in the morning he had bought large quantities of flour for his reserves, but upon opening the sacks he found the contents to be of dubious quality, and he was seeking to get rid of it as quickly as possible in a manner advantageous both to himself and to others. The airmen refused to speak with the baker about the estimate, which they did not understand, being above all unaccustomed to occupying themselves with such details. They gave instructions for the rolls to be baked immediately. To emphasize the fact that this was a matter of duty, the general even pounded his fist on the table, after which, considering the matter closed, he ordered the baker to leave.

The pharmacist appeared requesting a special allocation of dressing supplies from the government stores, in case for instance there were disturbances, which, he suggested, could not be ruled out in view of the influx of outsiders. His application appeared to have a legal basis: he backed it up with the argument that victims of disturbances never pay for their own treatment. In such a case, he was unwilling to cover the costs from his own pocket; and the general was forced to admit that there was no reason why he in particular should be expected to put himself out. Since the pharmacist knew which storeroom the dressing materials were kept in, the necessary keys were brought from the custodian's office and the door was officially opened. But the storeroom proved to be empty; there was only one solitary packet of bandages lying in a corner, and in place of sterile gauze, on the shelf they found a carton of chocolate bars, one of which moreover had been opened; someone had taken a bite out of it and wrapped it back up in crumpled silver foil.

The third person to enter the director's office was the notary. Cognizant of the fact that the resolution of his problem did not lie within the purview of the officials, he merely wished to report the disappearance of his son. He quoted the policeman, who had said there was nothing he could do in the matter. At this point one of the airmen, perhaps the one who was continually yawning, recalled that a moment ago as he was looking out the window he had seen two boys, a bigger one and a smaller one, crossing the roof of one of the neighboring buildings. The general listened attentively. He took the worried father respectfully by the elbow and led him to the window. For a short while everyone stared intently at the roofs. But there were no boys up there. The information given by the yawning officer seemed vague and not particularly plausible, and he might even have been thought to have imagined it. And so no progress was made in the notary's case, and his anxiety went unassuaged.

The baker too was in a quandary. He couldn't decide whether it was better for his business to make as few of the aforementioned rolls as possible, or if it made more sense to use up all the flour at once. He could bake only a small amount, just enough to satisfy the general's order, but if after the director came back it turned out that the authorities would refund the costs, he would be left with the bitter regret of having missed the opportunity to liquidate the whole lot – all those damned stockpiles of adulterated flour that he had mistakenly bought. On the other hand, the baker was worried that if he used up all of his poor-quality supplies and the refugees ate everything, and then the authorities refused to reimburse him, it would be a complete waste of the money he had spent so rashly that morning, in the grip of the prevailing panic. In the end, caution led him to bake only a small batch of rolls exclusively for the children from the orphanage. The airmen were said to have supplemented this gift generously by distributing one bar of chocolate per child; word of this spread quickly, preceding the handout itself. Upon hearing about the chocolate, certain of the locals tapped their foreheads to indicate the absurdity of the notion, as they had when the taxicabs were supposed to come, and they asked sarcastically if the chocolate too would be American. Others actually already knew it was.

But all the same, it did not appear. No one was able to explain where it had gotten to. It had vanished and that was all there was to it. The clerks were left with only a single bar, the one that had been opened and bitten into; this was plainly insufficient for the children and it was better to give it to the custodian, as a reward for his labors. And the only thing to come of it was that some of the more impetuous orphans began arguing about whether the chocolate that had passed them by had had a flavored filling or not. Those who knew best of all began giving out kicks. Others did not long remain in their debt, because they too were disappointed. In the view of the local residents, the orphanage children should have understood that what they did not have anyway beforehand could never truly belong to them. They were expected to stand in an orderly line and quietly take one roll each from the basket. But things happened differently. The stronger ones elbowed their way to the front unceremoniously, paying little heed to the black mourning armbands they wore on their sleeves. Because of the rolls, though also perhaps as a result of the chocolate, something had gotten into those children; their eyes shone as if in a fever. They cheated, came back when it was not their turn, and reached into the basket two or even three times. And before the last child in line had received his ration, the first ones, to the general indignation, began throwing rolls at one another, right under the nose of the baker, his family and neighbors, the policeman, the concierges, and the residents watching from behind lace curtains.

In the face of such a scandal, the baker dropped the basket. His own magnanimity stuck in his craw, since instead of the thankfulness he deserved he had found himself mocked. If I am him, I feel doubly deceived: first because of the flour, and second because of my feelings. One would have expected the hungry to be satisfied with what the full refused to eat. That whoever is fed out of pity would not make demands – the quality of the flour being none of their business. That a hungry child, especially, would gladly accept a roll. A rumor started circulating that the orphans were evidently not going hungry. They ought to, then. That would cure them of an arrogance unseemly in their situation, and would teach them respect for bread. The residents responded to this wicked ingratitude with a pained sigh and a vertical furrow of concern on their brow, as the rolls kept hitting the pavement with a dull thud, as if the baker had simply made rocks. Crushed by the burden of this moment, he pushed among the children and began taking back his rolls, snatching them from dirty hands. And one of the rocks flying to and fro overhead happened to strike him on the temple. His white baker's apron was instantly soiled with blood. Those nearby called for a doctor. Yet from the very beginning there was no mention of a doctor living on the square or practicing here. Situations requiring medical intervention were not anticipated at all. The dazed baker was led across the middle of the square directly to the pharmacy. The refugees parted silently for his escort in their grammar school overcoats, lowering their gaze at the accusatory stares. Up till this moment they had been complaining about the cordon and the turned-off faucet, but what they saw now was much plainer – the goodwill, the ingratitude, the blood. When the baker reappeared his wound was already dressed, red slowly seeping through the bandage round his head.

Since the orphanage children refused to say which of them had thrown the roll, under the supervision of the order guard each one received a whack of the birch on their hands. The school custodian was selected to carry out the punishment, since the birch belonged to him and he was adept in its use. True, the orphans cheated insolently in this matter too. The smallest ones presented themselves first, but then amid shouting and crying they went back a second and third time, continually pushed to the front of the line by the older, stronger children, as before without any regard for the faded signs of mourning on the sleeves of their little jackets. Justice was painful and at the same time not especially discriminating; the custodian did not concern himself with counting the blows to the hands, but only did what he had been ordered to by those more important than himself. What else could matter to him? The most cunning orphans thrust their hands into their pockets, and in this way got off scot-free. All around, so much anger had accumulated that someone had to be punished, if only for the crash, for the morning panic and the shoddy goods available in wholesale quantities on the black market. Who was supposed to carry the tribulations of the whole world, if not the orphanage? And in accordance with the universal rule, the tribulations of the orphanage were in turn borne by the weakest children – those who could find no one less important than themselves on whom to cast the shared burden.

The commotion roused the mongrel from a blissful doze. Hiding in some dark corner, he had already managed to digest the sausage he snaffled in the morning at the risk of life and limb. He crept out of his hiding place, stretched, gave a wag of his tail, and went to evacuate his bowels in the middle of the sidewalk, right in front of the government offices, after which he promptly bolted. Nothing here belongs to the mongrel – neither the stone of the pavement nor the slabs of the sidewalk. It is for this reason alone that he believes the whole square is ownerless just like himself, and that he can do anything he likes here. Only those who have principled rules concerning ownership submit willingly to the necessary restrictions. For them, the order separating them from all filth is sacred. It's obvious that it is easy to step in excrement if the eye has avoided looking at it in revulsion. So it was quickly smeared across the entire sidewalk, right in the spot where, in the morning, coins had spilled from the newsboy's pockets and vanished in the twinkling of an eye. Soon it was trodden in by everyone in turn: the air force general, the major, the captain, the lieutenant, and the commander of the order guard; and each of them cursed under his breath and looked about in search of anything whatsoever on which he could wipe the sole of his boot.

The shock was all the nastier because it happened to the airmen at lunchtime, just as they were getting ready for a good meal, their mouths watering at the mere thought of a white tablecloth, sparkling porcelain, and crystal-clear glassware. Their appetizing picture was befouled. But the lunch they had ordered ahead of time was awaiting them, and there was no reason to cancel it. Quite the opposite, the commander's thoughts were continually circling round the meal, amid fears that some unexpected event would render it impossible. The square on which the airmen had found themselves in the early morning, no one knew how or why, all of a sudden became indescribably repugnant to them, and that which was most slippery in it seemed to match the color of the plaster. They could no longer imagine anything more squalid than ochre. But still, as guests they followed on behind the commander of the guard. They entered the café at number one, which had been closed to ordinary customers since the morning, yet was open to certain people all along. The proprietor had still not been in touch, and over time the waiter had grown used to the idea that he never would. For although the license was issued in the name of a front man, the actual owner was the director of the local government offices – the very fellow who had disappeared without a trace.

A pronounced stench accompanied the commander and his guests into the café. As soon as they took their places at the table, the obliging, lisping waiter took their boots to be cleaned. Sitting at the table in their socks, they finally felt a sense of relief. They ate with relish the special dish not mentioned on the menu: pork knuckle with cabbage. They also enjoyed the chocolate mousse, which, like the pork knuckle, they owed to the waiter's resourcefulness. Everyone ate as much as he could without worrying if he would later be able to get up from his seat. It was all on the house. Nevertheless, the commander of the guard found the energy to try on the general's greatcoat, seemingly just as a joke. Because of his rank, the general served himself first from the various dishes, and led the way in over-eating and overdrinking. The moment he started to laugh, a button popped and his uniform jacket opened over his belly, showing the world his white undershirt. The general's button was located by the adjutant in the semidarkness under the table and was wrapped solicitously in a paper napkin.

The greatcoat hung on the commander of the guard as if it had been made to measure; it looked unquestionably better than on the general even, and the commander glanced uneasily towards the officers, unable to comprehend why they too were laughing fit to burst. During the short moment he had had the coat on, his eyes had glowed with a gold-tinted metallic gleam, as if they had always belonged to the braided collar. Confident in his appearance, which inspired benevolence along with an appropriate admixture of respect, and which inclined the residents of the apartment buildings to see in him a model of noble courage and pure intentions, the commander of the guard felt that the golden sheen was his due. After all, he was the one that maids had crushes on, he was the one the grammar school pupils looked up to, he was the one wished well by old men watching out from behind their lace curtains. For a moment he imagined that the general would present him with the greatcoat out of gratitude for all he had done. Why wouldn't he, especially if he could order as many coats of this kind as he wished? But what if, in the place he came from, there was not even one other such coat? So let him at least forget to take the coat with him when he flew off in the helicopter. It did not seem likely; one couldn't really count on his being so absentminded. The general's appearance also inspired respect, hinting at an iron will, experience, and a presence of mind that in the past had saved him more than once from mortal danger – otherwise he would not be sitting here at the table. One moment more, one more portion of chocolate mousse and one more glass, and he himself would start to recount the story. But what if the commander of the guard enlisted the help of the waiter? What if the latter agreed to take the greatcoat from the rack at a crucial moment and hide it somewhere?

However, first the helicopter would have to arrive, and there was still no sign of it. Was it not expected after lunch? The snow clouds had not dispersed but, on the contrary, had thickened. The airmen considered "after lunch" to mean more or less the same as "before dinner," so everything was in the best possible order. By the time dessert came, they had already recovered their spirits and wished to have some fun before their departure. But what was it they really wanted? They weren't interested in the billiard table of polished wood with its little pyramid of ivory balls arranged on the dark green baize. They would probably have preferred a noisy pinball machine with flashing colored lights, like the one in the air force mess where for years they had killed time in their off-duty hours. The officers were looking for pleasing distractions. But the commander couldn't even show them a good movie: the cinema projector had been removed, along with the rows of seats upholstered in threadbare plush, and the auditorium was filled with neatly piled sacks of quicklime, sand, and plaster that were evidently waiting for remodeling work to begin. So after a few more rounds, all they could do would be to have the waiter fetch a gramophone and then dance for a while, one airman with another, one officer with another, to the sound of the fox-trot. To amuse the company the youngest of them, the general's adjutant, might put on, for example, a lady's hat with a feather, procured from goodness knows where.

In the meantime, the inquisitive children from the orphanage had gathered at the window of the café and, unnoticed, their noses flattened against the pane, were avidly watching the spectacle: first the silverware maneuvering about the plates, then the fascinating remains of the chocolate mousse in a glass serving bowl, which eventually, to the astonishment of the audience, was shifted to the edge of the table to make room in the middle. The commander of the guard laid a paper napkin in its place and drew something on it for the airmen, who leaned forward intently. The general was enjoying a cigar and condescendingly watching the movements of the pen out of the corner of his eye. In the middle of the napkin there was a crooked circle. It was marked with numbers like the face of a clock. Above the twelve there appeared the word "offices," and beneath the six, "school." The number one was underlined twice, and a curved arrow led from it to the seven. At the seven the simple drawing grew more complicated. The dark depths of a gateway opened up here, cutting into the circumference of the circle; right next to it, in a jagged line, the outline of kitchen steps led upward to the right door. That was the best place to have the general's button sewn back on, and also for any other services they might require. The personal presence of the commander could be awkward; it would be sufficient to mention his name.

For a moment the pencil hovered undecidedly over the napkin. If I am the young man whose gaze is fixed on the general's greatcoat, I must just have remembered how she wouldn't let me go. She clung to my cuff, weeping, and when I gave it a tug, she almost tore it off. She needed a single sobering blow to the cheek; after that she calmed down at once. On second thought, he could safely assume that she was stupid and submissive enough not to make any more fuss: the wily old general would know how to handle her. The abbreviation "x 1" probably meant that they should climb only one flight of stairs, though it could also have indicated that the airmen ought to go to number seven one by one, and never in a group. So the major would follow the general, then would come the captain, with the young adjutant last. The commander put away his pencil, raised his honest steel gray eyes to the general and, standing from the table, placed the napkin in his hands.

It was then that he suddenly noticed half a dozen hungry pairs of eyes outside the window following his every movement. The spectators huddled together were not content with observing him as, having eaten so much he was fit to burst, he drew on the napkin, furtively suppressing a belch. They would have preferred him to go on eating rather than scribbling on napkins. They waited impatiently for the appearance of further courses, being unsated with the ones they had already seen.

They would have wanted to see other delicious morsels raised on his fork, so as once again to devour them with their gaze until they disappeared into the pink mouth beneath the neatly trimmed mustache. A rap on the windowpane gave mild expression to the commander's irritation, but it did not scare the mob away; quite the opposite, they responded by making faces and giggling impudently. There was no one around to drive them back behind the iron ring of the tracks.

If the commander of the guard had had his boots on, he would have run out on the spot and dealt with them himself. It would have been enough, he believed, to grab one of them by the scruff of the neck and give him a few kicks on the shin; the rest would have quieted down at once and would not have said another word. In the meantime, the general and the major have already gotten back their boots, which have been polished till they gleam; the captain is just getting ready to pull his on, and the adjutant will be next. If I am the leader of the guard, I demand my boots! This instant! Yet the boots are still in the closet by the cloakroom, next to the adjutant's, last in line for being cleaned. The waiter would not dare bring them as they are, dirty and smelly; he prefers to grovel tearfully and offer endless apologies. And so minutes go by, and the spectators outside the window, relishing the commander's helplessness, torment him by aping his gestures, laughing as they shake their fists. In response to the curses spilling from the commander's lips, barely audible murmurs of reassurance come from the back room. So the commander starts pounding on the window; a moment longer and he'd be brought to his senses by the sound of breaking glass he knows so well. And the children scatter. They run away and hide in courtyards, attics, and who knows where else. If I am the commander, I have my men to thank for all this. They evidently all went off home the moment their superior officer was out of sight – for, extraordinary as it seems, they too were eager for their lunch.

The waiter, a figure of the most beggarly cut, is of too little significance here to be able to make amends for the indignity he has caused the commander – the regrettable moment when he left him in his stockinged feet in front of an insolent derisive rabble. And because of this, the long-awaited lunch with the officers went unappreciated. The admiring and grateful question of where the waiter had obtained the pork knuckle, and how he had miraculously been able to marinate it and roast it, would never be uttered. If anything at all here could be made right, it would only happen if the waiter were forced to take all of the mockery upon himself, to be submerged in it, to sink in ridicule without mercy and without end. When the boots are finally brought, then, the commander will grab them by the uppers and for a long time will assail this figure, who in his consternation will be lisping even more than usual, until the offense is washed away in blood. It will drip from a cut over the eye onto the black tailcoat and the white shirt front. The airmen pretend they are involved in their game of billiards, their backs turned, rather than watch this scene, which reminds them only too much of the barracks. The balls click against one another unconvincingly and miss the pockets. A word of gratitude will be found for the commander, but not until he is pulling on the boots, for only then will they sense it's finally over, and breathe a sigh of relief. Their thanks will sound rather offhand considering the care with which they have been treated, the cordial hospitality and the astonishing lavishness of the meal. The reserve with which the airmen shake hands with the commander is especially painful to him, though on the other hand he understands that he ought not to bear a grudge.

Alas, nothing has gone as planned, and it's no surprise he has grown solemn. With one more longing glance into the cloakroom, at the gold-trimmed greatcoat which would have been so much more effective than his own jacket in setting the tone of his relations with the world, the leader of the guard sets out on his business, not noticing that his boots still smell. Only one course of action remained to him, one last resort: he must now gather his subordinates, line them up, and call to account the first one at hand. Returning from their homes, the guardsmen assembled in the school yard. Given soup and chops by their mothers, they had no excuses. All the more so because after lunch barely half of them had returned to their unit. What had happened to the rest? Had their mothers kept them at home and made them do their homework? If they started doing what their mothers said, the whole lot of them would end up deserting.

That was what he was afraid of. For the moment, though, they stood in a shortened but orderly double line in the grammar school yard, while he stormed back and forth in front of them, furious at those he could no longer reach. The longer he raged, the angrier he became. As he screamed till he was out of breath, meaningful pauses came of their own accord. In this way it cost no effort whatsoever to imitate the harsh tone of the radio broadcast. But the cadences of his speech were drowned out by dance music. Fox-trots could be heard coming from the café, where the gramophone with its big trumpet had been turned up to full volume.

By early afternoon someone had already picked up the chalk-and-plaster fragments left after the incident that some time ago had interrupted the distribution of the rolls, and had put them to use. The first scrawl to deface the walls had appeared on the façade of the cinema. It was a question mark with a provocatively curving belly, devoid of any context whatsoever. Since no one knew what it referred to specifically, it brought everything without exception into question, including the lace curtains in the windows, the ornamental railings, the widely accepted principle that one's fingernails ought to be clean, and the dignity of the life being led all around. Through its suggestiveness, the question mark became vulgar and offensive in and of itself. The guards were ordered to scratch it out, making use of their unlimited access to school supplies of chalk. From that moment, for a long while they were kept busy, because question marks kept popping up here, there, and everywhere. Yet no one was caught red-handed. At least four such marks blighted the front of the government offices alone, one standing out mockingly beneath the damaged emblem. Two could be seen at number seven, a larger one and a smaller one, joined together in a single visibly obscene figure. The orphanage children, who were sticking their noses into everything, may well have preferred to write plainly and simply that, for example, here at number seven a young lady went with a young man. But that would have taken too many letters. A question mark is the easiest thing to scribble in haste, when the writer is all set to scram at a moment's notice. Exposed to the public view, it immediately takes on a shared meaning that is allusive in the most general sense. The guards ran from place to place, smudged in chalk from head to foot, till the last question mark had vanished, and all the buildings around the square were covered near ground level with a rash of expressive blotches that would never let anyone forget that here anything could be called into question.

In the meantime the orphanage children were already busy with something else. Seizing the opportunity, they were prowling the unwatched courtyards while the concierges were minding the front of their buildings. In threes and fours, they hurriedly emptied the trash cans they found there. Up to their knees in the contents, they sought remnants of food. They picked out kitchen scraps and stuffed themselves. The things they ate upset their stomachs, and soon they were dirtying entranceways, landings, and anyplace they happened to be. It was as if they were deliberately provoking the residents, especially those in the buildings overlooking the street, who, according to the universally respected order of things, had the right to give a wide berth to all that was revolting, including by-products of the pure elixir of their life. To see excrement at every step was a true plague, compared with which the isolated incident involving the drifting smell and the ochre smear on the sidewalk was a matter of no consequence.

But if I am one of the residents watching from behind a lace curtain, I realize that the problems did not begin with the children from the orphanage, nor do they end with them. The very presence of the newcomers living right there on the street is already scandalous to me. It's hard to remain calm as one watches them settle on their suitcases, each of them arranging a small area of the square with their own belongings. One is snoring as he sits and dozes; another has taken off his shoe and sock and is examining his blisters. The body stinks – this truth too must finally be uttered. Its dirty nature cannot be kept under control with continuous hygienic procedures involving hot water, soap, brushes large and small, handkerchiefs, nail files, jars of vaseline, and bottles of scent. All of this takes up a great deal of space. There is a need for closets, shelves, and cabinets. Thus the body, deprived not only of a roof over its head but also of everything else, cannot expect sympathy, but on the contrary it must become an offense against decorum, the disgrace of the neat and respectable community of residents. Then what on earth are they to say when, casually multiplied by the hundreds, the body swells into a crowd. If, then, I am any one of the residents, I feel sorry only for the concierge who is tugging the policeman's sleeve to complain about the disorder.

The clerks from the government offices maintained that since it was not possible to get rid of the refugees at once, temporary solutions needed to be found. For example, the construction of latrines. The concierges ought to help out in this endeavor, since they too would make use of them. The concierges preferred to lend their spades to the provisional authorities, who could have the refugees do the digging themselves. The only problem was that no one could agree on where the pit should be dug. The one place that everyone thought of was the flower bed in the middle of the square, which may already have been doomed to destruction; it had probably been trampled long ago, plowed up by heels and flattened under suitcases. But the commander merely waved his hand dismissively. In his view there was no point in wasting resources. Instead of turning the flower bed into a latrine, it would be better to spare it and plant new flowers once the situation was normalized. The refugees are forbidden from entering the courtyards, and there is no point in revoking this order without good reason. A state of affairs as perturbing as the present one is by its nature transitory, and so as the commander sees it, things will soon resolve themselves even without a latrine. The policeman, buttonholed by proponents of both solutions, has no intention of taking sides. He listens indifferently to the concierges' complaints and the residents' advice, merely nodding his head at the order guard's loss of face.

The commander still has no idea that his men are being laughed at behind their backs. He does not spare himself; he and his guards do what they can to improve the situation. Searching constantly for a good way out, he thought for some time about the entrance to the storm drain, as a literal exit. This new idea brought hope that it would be possible to lead the crowd out of the square, and perhaps even to send them off for good into the unknown, so that someone else, somewhere else, would have to deal with the whole problem. The commander sent two people to lift the iron grille and take a look inside. This they did without delay. But, as they ran up to report, under the grille no drain was to be seen. There was only packed sand, in which the trademark of the ironworks was imprinted like a seal.

During this time someone well hidden from view had the leader of the guard in the sights of a revolver. It was the bigger of the two boys who had been sitting together like the best of friends on the roof of the government offices, concealed among the chimneys. He followed the commander right and left with the barrel, from time to time removing his glasses, which kept misting over. At these moments he had to do something with the revolver. Thrusting it into the waistband of his pants, a rather uncomfortable operation, he took out his handkerchief and wiped the spectacles. His pal plucked at his shoulder, asking for the gun, and though he was smaller he evidently expected to be given it in the end. In the meantime, the streetcar had pulled up at the stop and had unexpectedly shielded the order guard and its commander. The barrel of the gun, trembling slightly in the older boy's hand, moved away from the streetcar at random, up to the level of the second floor, and all at once in the sights there was the silhouette of a woman standing in the window of an apartment at number seven – a mother of children and wife of the notary. The instant her profile appeared, her son hurriedly handed over the gun, as if it were burning him. Was he afraid that the finger could pull the trigger of its own accord, before the head forbade it? In the hands of the younger boy, the news seller from number eight, the barrel luckily swung away from the window and selected a new target, for the boy's thoughts too were drifting towards different regions. The mongrel, principal cause of the wrongs he had suffered, had appeared in the sights. His finger on the trigger, he followed the dog's every move, biting his lip harder and harder, till finally he lowered the gun and cursed, his voice breaking, because for some reason he was unable to shoot.

If events take a different turn, towards more merciful solutions than could have been expected, it is only because the rules, like everything else in the vicinity, are not functioning properly. But even if they sometimes go wrong, they still remain permanently inscribed in the background, like the lines simulating perspective on the plywood boards: an immovable and always current system of reference. The censored fragments sawed out of the boards will change nothing here either – even if the lines are removed, they continue to be imagined. As for the gun, it could only belong to the notary. It was the son, impatiently awaited by his mother, who had taken it from their home. Some time ago he had managed to sneak in the back door while his father was gone and had removed the revolver from the latter's desk drawer. As he tiptoed down the long hallway to the kitchen door, shoes in hand, he could not help noticing that the always open door to the maid's room was now closed. For a moment he even stood outside it and listened intently, a look of astonishment on his round, boyish face. In the end he peeked through the keyhole. He could see a student cap tossed carelessly on a stool. Then he was able to go unhurriedly into the kitchen, where lunch was going cold in the pots, waiting in vain for its time to come. He took a couple of chicken legs, wrapping them in the personals page of the newspaper.

Where the revolver in the drawer came from will never be established. It could have lain there dormant for years. When a warm human body comes close, a single moment suffices to wake it up. The gun's very shape is, for the hand, a meaningful sign. But meaningful in a special way that seems on the surface to be removed from reality, foreign to the innocent language of everyday things, for example, bread knives and soupspoons. Yet one touch is enough for all the fingers to know instantly where they belong and what this is about. The middle and ring fingers close around the grip; the index finger quickly finds the trigger. It's entirely possible that the revolver, by its nature a symbolic object, becomes literal only when it is brought to life by the sufferings of a secondary character, by his fevered and angry thoughts. Those thoughts too are looking for release, since no grievances or reparations have been provided for here, and no one knows what to do with such an excess of ill feeling. All one can do is drown in it.

It is impossible to combat the illicit weapons that have proliferated secretly, beyond the control assured by the invoices. Individual items surface at rare moments, in secluded corners, when a romance has turned imperceptibly into a crime story, a farce into a drama. On the basis of the invoices it's easy to declare the opposite belief, asserting that guns do not exist at all. It would have been better if this were true. If what was in circulation were only painted props made of wood and cardboard, with pretend bullets. But the secondary character, filled with festering resentment, will never be satisfied with this. He knows too much about things to be taken in. In the cylinder of the revolver taken from the drawer, fortunately, there is only a single round. This gun can be fired just once. But, as would be true anywhere, one shot will be enough to move things forward with a bang, in the least expected direction. On the other hand, there are many ways to prevent the shot even at the last moment, so long as the glint of an oxidized barrel is spotted in time. The gun is once again shaking in the hands of the older boy as he waits patiently for the streetcar to pull away and expose the school yard on which the commander is presently receiving reports from his men. The newsboy, his dirty cheeks streaked with tears, is greedily chewing a chicken leg. The notary's son is already starting to get bored. The streetcar remains at the stop outside the grammar school for so long that it eventually becomes clear it will never leave.

If I am the driver, I realized a while back that something is up. To begin with, I just stare through the windshield at the places where the rails are joined together, but then I get out of the car, determined to take a closer look. I see that the rails have not been fastened to the baseplates the way they should. Actually, there are no baseplates at all; the rails are barely held together with figures-of-eight twisted by hand out of thick wire and fixed in place with nuts. Unable to believe my eyes, I go up to the next joint. Its nuts have fallen out; someone evidently couldn't even be bothered to tighten the bolts properly. At the next joint the wire figure-of-eight is snapped. I prod the rail with the tip of my boot and watch it tip over. So that's how they laid the tracks! But who did it? That the driver cannot know. And when? Beforehand, that much is clear even to him. In the recent or distant past. In a past that seems, like cause and effect, to be linked to the present moment but does not belong to it at all. Just as the rails need wooden baseplates, the base of an agreed-upon past is needed by events, but only so as to stabilize their course. It holds them permanently on the right track and removes various doubts that otherwise might lead to a derailment. As long as it continues to do its job, the characters submit to the illusion that they understand the sense of everything in which they have become embroiled.

So it remains only to admit that at dawn the streetcar set off, emerging from nothingness – that is the whole truth, and there will be no other. All accomplished facts preceding this moment must do without scenery, without backdrops or props. They are something understood, partly optional, added to the story like a misleading footnote, a sham appendix to the memory allotted, for example, to the notary along with the three-piece suit, or to the streetcar driver together with his driver's cap. The moment this person got out to look at the tracks, it transpired that he wasn't even dressed appropriately in a costume made of uniform fabric, but was wearing a plain off-duty suit of imitation wool. And when it comes down to it, the truth is that had it not been for the pathetic surprise that jolted the streetcar from its rhythm of riding and stopping, bringing it to a halt at a random point on its orbit, a uniform would have been unnecessary all the way to the end. Nor would the embarrassing circumstance ever have come to light that the suit is poorly made: the jacket too tight, the pants with uneven legs, one too long, the other too short, while, as if out of mockery, the side seams are held together with tacking thread. So long as everything proceeded the way it was supposed to, through the windshield one could see only the service cap, and even that indistinctly. And as for the cap, nothing was wrong with it.

Confronted with the evidence, the driver is forced to accept that since the start of the day the streetcar has lacked any kind of solid support beneath its wheels, while at times it was loaded beyond all measure. If I am the driver, I toss a mocking question into the void: how could it all have held together the whole day? But there will be no reply. He can merely shake his head and purse his lips. Deeper down, around his diaphragm, something else is gathering that cannot be suppressed: a powerful, acrid wave of empty laughter. So the driver stands by the tracks, looks at the streetcar, and laughs like a madman till his cap falls from his head. There is no reason for him to return to his seat. But if he has not actually gone mad, sooner or later he'll calm down, grow solemn, pick up his cap, and dust it off. After looking into the emptiness of one's own fate, it is hard to push on.

An airman hurrying from the gateway of number seven bumped into the streetcar driver. He apologized without stopping even for a moment, because he was in a hurry to return to the café at number one, where the gramophone was still playing at full volume. Nothing got on the driver's nerves so much as those fox-trots, whose lively rhythms poked fun at his despondency. He walked up and down the car for a while, sitting in one place or another. Evidently not one of the many sitting and standing places was meant for him. He smoked a cigarette on the front platform, then wandered about next to the car, staring ever more distractedly now at the pantograph, now at the wheels, and now at the round zero, as if seeing it all for the first time. Then he began hesitantly to move away. His legs would have liked to take him home, but his mind could not decide which way it was supposed to be. So, walking off, he had to come back again, circle the streetcar, and head off at a brisk pace in the opposite direction. He looks down the streets leading off the square. Their pavement cannot be trodden upon. Every step is in vain, whichever way it leads. He can only aim a kick at a painted board and hear a dull, echoing thud in response. The distance is pure illusion – paint and plywood, nothing more. It's true that there is little space here. Perhaps other stories contain more room, but even so, there's no doubt that in each of them one would eventually come up against a wall, knocking one's forehead on a board upon which a distant prospect appears to extend. The driver kicks the backdrop over and again. He will keep kicking it furiously till a cardboard patch falls off and reveals a hole that has been sawed out. He'll manage to crawl through the hole; his cap will eventually vanish from sight. He is evidently destined to wander henceforth between stories, in the marshaling yards, amid the red-brick walls; to pass by the rusty platforms of mechanical hoists; to step on empty bottles abandoned in the grass. He will not find his way home, that much is certain. No road leads there.

THERE WAS ONE RUMOR AFTER ANOTHER concerning the disappearance of the director. Apparently, early in the morning he suffered a stroke on his way to work, the moment he heard about the putsch. His eyes flipped upward, then he fell headlong and did not get up. The ambulance, sirens blaring, took him no one knows where from or where to. He had also definitely been seen later on the square in the crowd of refugees: it was easier for him to hide in anonymity amongst them rather than take on an onerous struggle with the chaos brought about by the overthrow. Though on the other hand, as certain voices declared, chaos had reigned in the offices since time immemorial anyway; recent events had merely exposed it and revealed its dimensions to outsiders. From other, absolutely reliable sources it was known that around noon the director had been arrested at his home by order of the organizers of the putsch, who had to imprison supporters of the fallen regime. Yet on the other hand, it was also said that the new authorities pursued them in such a way that they would not be caught, and even made strenuous efforts to entice them over to their own side, offering cushy jobs that required nothing from them except an abandonment of all principles, an appropriate ruthlessness, and servile cynicism. The director had yielded to such a proposition, and for that reason he already had an office elsewhere, which by all accounts was much more imposing. And so even if it was true that in the early morning he had in fact had a stroke and had also been arrested, in light of further circumstances he could expect no sympathy. Most people, including the clerks, came to the conclusion that he had gotten what he deserved.

The residents of the apartment buildings were constantly listening to the radio in the hope that out of the turbid waters of upbeat news they would be able to filter out a long-awaited droplet that would reassure them about the future. Against the current of the meager trickle of official information there flowed ever newer rumors about approaching final resolutions. Now it was an imminent landing by the allies to bring liberation; now it was Kolchak's forces, which somewhere out in the world would occupy the capital before suppertime and reinstate the legitimate government; now it was a band of partisans, armed to the teeth and promising to save the country from anarchy; now an international peacekeeping force was going to intervene and persuade the dictatorship to step down; now it was the arrival of the Huns, after whose passage not one stone would be left upon a stone. Ideas remained in constant circulation, bouncing against one another like marbles, but common sense rightly believed in only one thing: that lunchtime had already come and gone.

The helicopter expected after lunch was already circling, it suddenly seemed to the guards. Though only its faint outline could be discerned in the overcast sky. The airmen glanced up and shrugged: clouds were amassing over the square and soon it would snow. Yet even if the helicopter were actually to come, where was it supposed to land? Now the commander of the guard had to solve the matter of the crowd occupying the entire expanse of the square – a problem that had already proved intractable for many hours. In fact, it seemed insoluble. The commander thought about it perpetually, as if in a fever, now inspired by the task of dreaming up a truly brilliant plan, now prey to irritation and disillusion. It would have seemed that the simplest thing was to lift the ban on crossing the line of the tracks and to disperse the crowd into the gateways of buildings as soon as the whir of helicopter blades was heard. But afterwards how could the refugees be pried from the courtyards, stairwells, and attics, and driven back onto the square? What sanctions could be imposed on the outsiders, and how could they be separated from the locals? What principle should be applied? The cut of their overcoats? The smell of mothballs? To put it differently, the commander did not know how to arrange things so that the square should be empty once again but that no one should be roaming the courtyards – that the crowd should disappear but not be freed. Temporary measures ought not to rule out a better solution when one was subsequently found. Various ideas were circulating on this subject too, but none of them seemed right. Even the simplest suggestion, involving the use of public transportation, was for obvious reasons impracticable. Nor was it at all clear where these people were to be sent, since it seemed beyond question that there was no place for them anywhere.

The waiter, meanwhile, was still trying to treat his wound,

stopping the bleeding with cold compresses. He had used up the entire stock of clean napkins from the back room of the café, and was already starting to worry about what he would say if he ended up after all having to explain this fact to the owner. He was of so little significance that there was no room for his problems. Because of the unexpected complication that had arisen, he had already begun to neglect his duties; he could not count on leniency. In this situation the easiest thing would be to relinquish wounded self-love like an additional piece of luggage when both one's hands are full. Forced to rely on his own resources, he shuffled restlessly about the back rooms without rhyme or reason, leaving bright streaks on the doorknobs and the paneling, and smearing dark red marks on the checkered floor tiles with the soles of his shoes. He was the very person who was supposed to clean up here – a character without any other functions, always available, and easiest of all to replace. Whereas those after whom he had to wash and sweep and launder tablecloths were for the café, just as for the whole world, the irreplaceable mainstay of the only order there was. The fox-trots blared out unsympathetically from the gramophone, driving the waiter with his suffering and his helplessness from the main dining room to the storeroom in the back, where his head continued to throb from the din. Had he been able, he'd have preferred to raise his head and join the merry uproar, laughing at everything along with those untouched by ill fortune. But no one ever saw him with his head raised. Out of occupational habit, he was stooped in a permanent bow. Whether he liked it or not, he could not repudiate this abased body to which he had been chained.

What if he did not stop bleeding? Since help for the baker had been found at the pharmacy, the waiter eventually went there as well. Too late. A card was stuck on the glass door announcing that the pharmacist had been called away on urgent business. The waiter could see out of only one eye; when that eye saw the pharmacy was closed, he turned pale. He sat on the step, determined never to move from that place. If he had died there someone would have had to remove the body, which would have been rather heavy and, with its decease, absolved of all responsibility. True, it was the only body he had, but death severs such attachments too. It was difficult for him to argue with the general belief that the birth of a child was more important. But he was angered by this obdurate bias on the part of the majority, its condescending pity for small pink beings whose vulnerability inspires hypocritical emotions, until they grow up and become ugly, turning drab like everything around them. The pity of the majority is reluctant to make sacrifices: custom dictates that its noble impulses are paid for by those it overlooks. Those who, for example, are entirely thrust aside in their drabness and have not even gained entry to the pharmacy. The waiter felt weak and for a moment he thought he was beyond help. But by good fortune the wound quite unexpectedly stopped bleeding; so he stood up and without further ado left to clean up the back rooms of the café and remove all traces of the embarrassing scenes of humiliation and fear he had experienced there. It was easy enough to take a damp cloth and wipe away the bloodstains from the floor and the door handles. Only the tailcoat would not come fully clean. That was a true wrong and a serious blow. It was hard to say whether the waiter would be able to hold on to his job in a dirty tailcoat. And if not – what would he wear, and what would he become?

If I am one of those respectable citizens casting occasional glances at the square from an upstairs window, I have been able to watch it all simultaneously: the waiter staggering to the pharmacy, the pharmacist elbowing his way through the crowd, and the woman who had begun to give birth. The birth was only to be expected, since for some time the pregnant woman had simply been lying amid the suitcases. Her screams came from somewhere in the middle of the square and were lost amid the hubbub of other voices. But from an upstairs window she could plainly be seen, laid out on her own overcoat, her eyes shut tight, gripping the hem of her raised skirt as she yielded to the violent contractions. It had fallen to her lot to give birth right here, so she could not count on being screened from the curiosity of those watching from above, each of whom would have declared at this moment that the need for privacy was alien to the refugees, who were devoid of culture and lacked self-respect. If I am watching from an upstairs window, I consider this birth to be very poorly timed, and I disapprove of the fact that the authorities permitted it to happen.

In the meantime the pharmacist, who was being reprimanded by the leader of the guard for causing a disturbance, but who was twice as old as him and furthermore indispensable in his role, grew angry and turned his back, cutting the discussion short. He knew enough to understand that the forces of nature cannot be squeezed into the boundaries imposed by bureaucratic injunctions, nor can they be held in check by slogans about public order. At this point one might ask suspiciously where, in the pharmacist's opinion, had the forces of nature come from in this crowded space surrounded on all sides by a backdrop painted on plywood boards. Yet those forces did their work in the space of less than a quarter of an hour. Before the snow began to fall, the first cry of a baby was heard. It was all over. A child had been born, according to the rumor that quickly made the rounds of the square and the apartment buildings. But no one had seen the child with his own eyes. The moment it had been given a diaper and wrapped in blankets, someone had passed it to someone else, and that was that. There was no way for the pharmacist to be in control of everything at the same time. The circumstances required too much of him; instead of the requisite knowledge, he possessed only a faint memory of dissection exercises carried out many years before as a student, and the vague recollection of illustrations from an obstetrics atlas he had once happened to glance at. His sleeves rolled up, covered to the elbows in blood and fluids, he was just reaching for a towel.

It was quite possible that nothing aside from a birth could have moved this crowd, which since morning had grown only too familiar with misfortune. And indeed the crowd was enthralled by the birth, and horrified by the disappearance of the child. Everyone who was able took part in the search; eye-witnesses to the birth felt especially duty bound to do what they could, so they brusquely demanded information from the blind man. For he was the one who, for no apparent reason, had pushed among them at the most important moment and had obscured their line of sight. He had been forced to hand his cane over to the guards, and without this indicator his condition was not sufficiently obvious for them to leave him alone. Through his dark glasses he could not have seen anything, so he recalled nothing either, even when he was shaken angrily by the lapels of his overcoat. He jerked himself free, not understanding what they wanted of him, and clutching his instrument case ever more firmly. This was suspicious, and so his interrogators did not rest till they had wrenched the case from his grip and looked inside. It contained a violin. Amid the ensuing tussle it almost got smashed. Finally left in peace, for a long time the blind man passed his fingers over the instrument, stroking it and kissing it, still unable to believe it had survived. Everyone else, though, would have preferred to see the violin go to hell and the missing child found. Ignoring all that was going on around her, the mother was demanding her baby. First in a whisper, seemingly exhausted by the exertions of labor, then soon afterwards in a terrible scream that gave people gooseflesh. Since the infant was nowhere to be found, they started urging the pharmacist to give her an injection to calm her down. In the end he had to comply. He liked to think of himself as a conscientious fellow, so he did not withhold the necessary medications from his own personal supplies, but he did so reluctantly and bitterly, mentally calculating how very much his own decency had already cost him.

The father of the family shouldered his way through the crowd like a madman. He thrust people aside left and right, looking into baskets and bundles. His three other children trotted along behind him, the youngest clinging to his coat so as not to get lost; he was preceded by rumors of a missing baby. His desperate search led him in ever-widening circles, and more and more people joined in; after the father passed by, the crowd rippled in a manner even more wearing than during the scourge of the street trade. It was for this reason that the commander of the guard laid hands on him in person and twisted his arm back so as to force him in a different direction.

This was no time for foolishness. The line of guards in their grammar school coats with the official armband on the sleeve was already pushing the crowd towards the cellars beneath the cinema, of necessity lashing out with their sticks, for otherwise they would never have managed to drive anyone away from their belongings. Although the residents watching from the windows of their apartments had complete respect for property, violence was justified by a higher need: if these people had been permitted to burden themselves with their luggage again, the evacuation would have taken forever. True, during the operation the guards were laughing. And in this way, some people laughing, others frightened and anxious, together they gradually lost all their confidence and were helplessly plunged in the same despair.

As far as orders were concerned, all was plain: the center of the square had to be cleared immediately. Otherwise the helicopter presently circling in the clouds overhead would never have been able to land. It would have had to fly away empty, returning where it came from. Sending the helicopter back – which would be entirely the fault of the crowd, and of that sluggish inertia so hard to overcome – would have turned the whole hierarchy upside down. No amount of compassion for second-rate padded overcoats could have justified disrespect for an officer's uniform; in this matter every one of the locals admitted that the commander of the guard was right. In the end he had found it extraordinarily easy to recover the free space, despite the fact that for so many hours it had seemed an impossible task. All that had been needed was to remove the bundle of keys to the cinema from the photographer's drawer. In the space of a short moment there wasn't a soul on the square; all that remained of the newcomers were the ownerless suitcases. Anyone who wanted could have taken them. And all those who had given their stockpiles of cigarettes to the refugees in return for a piece of porcelain now felt cheated and robbed. The recent presence, turned so suddenly into absence, was remarked on with all the more malice because while the crowd had still been encamped on the square, not all the locals had managed to express their opinion about its ways, make appropriate comparisons, or conclude that they were savages from goodness knows where and that destruction would inevitably ensue from their presence here. All at once it had become too late to say one's piece on this subject. No sooner had the square been vacated than to everyone's astonishment it turned out that the flower bed had survived unscathed. By some miracle the crowd had kept off it, not trampling it even when they were retreating under the blows of batons. If I am one of the local residents, in my opinion the guards deserve a special commendation for this circumstance. When it was all over, the policeman emerged from the gateway of number seven clutching a half-eaten chicken wing. The first snowflakes were falling on the yellow flowers.

And now the rounded shape of the helicopter suddenly loomed out of the swirling clouds, stirring up a wind that almost blew the flags off the façades of the buildings, and knocked hats and grammar school caps from heads as if they weighed nothing at all. In the café the helicopter's roar had been recognized at once, from the moment it began to superimpose itself over the blaring sounds of the fox-trot. The gramophone abruptly fell silent. The airmen hurried out onto the square, just in time to watch the helicopter land on the basalt cobblestones in front of the local government offices. Its blades spun slower and slower till they came to a complete stop. The general was the last to emerge from the café; he was not wearing his greatcoat or even his cap. Evidently he did sometimes forget things after all, thought the commander of the guard, and his heart pounded with joy that he would now have the coat, and the cap as well, as an unexpected bonus he could never have dared count on. Wearing the general's cap and greatcoat, he would have everyone under his command, including the pharmacist; the latter would regret having treated him like an idiot. The policeman too, who from now on would be obliged to stand at attention when he saluted him, and to deliver written reports. For what were threadbare suits, an ill-fitting police jacket, shabby local autumn coats, an overcoat with a fur collar, or even his own well-cut jacket with the metal insignia on the lapel compared to the general's woolen cloth and gold braid? Not to mention dark padded overcoats from goodness knows where – numberless, shabby, and of no value whatsoever.

At the last moment a junior clerk ran from the government offices with the portable shortwave radio, which had been left behind. He intended to hand it to the airmen through the door of the helicopter, but it was too late, as the blades were already turning again. The pilot, barely visible behind the frost-covered windshield, wore a leather flying jacket and dark glasses. The helicopter's sides were coated with a thin layer of ice. But one only had to look more closely for a moment to see that the outside of the fuselage was made out of sheets of thick corrugated cardboard covered with silver foil. This realization alone gave rise to all kinds of doubts. It was hard to imagine how the helicopter could have survived as it flew high over the earth, perhaps from far away, with no ground beneath its landing skids, in dense clouds; or how the pilot had prevented it from crashing the moment it took off. But the officers in this story were paid their salary not for flying so much as for knowing how to refrain from asking questions and how to get by without answers. The ease with which they were prepared at any moment to hop into the cockpit, and their impressive immunity to doubt, were valued highly. The airmen earned their livelihood from not being tied to the ground, either by attachment or by fear. Unquestionably it was only their unparalleled nonchalance that allowed them to stay up in the air along with their aircraft. They were unsuited to anything else. It was quite possible that over there, in their own story, they flew exclusively in dummy craft like this one. Piloting them with a sure hand, they performed rolls, loops, and spirals whose frivolous elegance convinced the viewer that everything was in perfect order, and that the only thing needed to fly was sang-froid and an unshaken confidence in one's lucky star. And indeed nothing more was necessary. As the commander stood with the guard of honor and saluted the helicopter, as the order was given and the guardsmen gave a farewell cheer, and the residents of the apartment buildings, who had come out onto the sidewalks, began waving their handkerchiefs – the helicopter suddenly rose into the air and vanished in the clouds. Only one piece of corrugated cardboard, its foil covering torn and aflutter, fell from the sky right at the onlookers' feet.

Then the snow began coming down in earnest, continually covering up traces. Its pure white buried the poorly constructed streetcar tracks and the smeared excrement. It went on for a good quarter of an hour or longer, till the supplies in the clouds were used up. When it had all fallen the clouds themselves disappeared, but now there came a harsh frost. Those who know about the explosion that rocked the marshaling yards in the morning will not be surprised by the frost: the compressor that by chance survived the crash had been turned on after the transformer was repaired. Impenetrable forests began to sprout on windowpanes, and this unexpected vegetation, silver like the coins lost earlier by the unfortunate newsboy from number eight, cut the residents of the apartments off from events taking place on the square. Though in fact, on the square hardly anything was happening. The commander's footprints could be seen cutting across the middle, from when he had crossed to the café to get the general's greatcoat. The steps were long and brisk, because the commander was fetching something that might as well have belonged to him. But in the cloakroom there was no sign of the coat. In the place where it had hung before, a painful void stung the eyes. The waiter had gone too. His ruined tailcoat remained, hanging over the back of a chair. There was no one in the café and no one in the back rooms. Only the gramophone with its big trumpet recalled the fact that not long ago a party had been going on: a record was still spinning silently on the turntable. It was an expensive model of a kind that no one in the neighborhood owned. It too had probably come from the refugees' belongings. For some unknown reason a woman's hat with a feather lay in the corner. The front door, which the student had not bothered to close properly, was banging in the wind. Icy gusts made the white tablecloth flap; at the edge of the table there was still a pile of dirty dishes left over from the shared lunch – empty glasses, plates with scraps of pork knuckle, and dried smudges of chocolate mousse in the glass bowl. The unfinished tea had gone cold in the cups.

The student's uncertain footsteps zigzagged along by the walls of the apartment buildings as he returned with nothing. His steps mingled with others left a moment before by someone quicker than him. The snow, which was gradually easing up, still covered them partially till they became entirely illegible. In places the indistinct outline of a shoe looked more like the imprint of a dog's paw. At the corner it even took on the shape of a raptor's talons, only to turn back into the shape of a regular sole. Following this trail, the student found himself in the school yard at the very moment when his men were raising a cheer in honor of the new commander of the order guard, who held the rank of general. The general had a fearful scar over his eye and in his speech the bluster of the leading character whose privileges he had always lusted after. Would he now wish to take revenge for his earlier humiliations, for example, a certain episode in which he was beaten about the head with a pair of boots? But what boots? All his indignities had been eclipsed by the dazzling braid, along with the attached memory of a golden string of successes adorning his whole life. The stern marshal with the piercing gaze in the picture frame would not be ashamed of such a general. Even the fact that he had a slight lisp was of no special significance, since from now on all he had to do was issue commands, and commands always sound convincing. The command "left turn!" sufficed for all the guards to turn their backs on the student in an instant; there was nothing but a clicking of heels and the creaking of the snow. Even if he'd tried to protest against this turn of events, now it was unlikely he, as a mere civilian shivering from the cold, could ever shout over the singing of the guards, which, when the order was given, had risen above the school yard immediately following the cheers. An army belt strapped round his ordinary jacket, the student looked rather foolish. His clothing hung shapelessly on his stooping shoulders. Only the general's eye rested on him briefly. It was a cold, mocking gaze that was hard to endure, so the student turned and walked away.

In the morning it had seemed that the thread of his story line needed simply to be tightened for it to keep all the other ones in check. But now, frayed and snapped off in the middle, it is of no more use. If he only could, the student himself would rip it out of the warp of the story, toss it down, and trample it underfoot in fury and contempt. Betrayed by himself as well as by others, he had no one else to count on. That was why, as he left the grammar school, his footprints could lead only to the apartment building at number five. On the way he stopped once and from under a layer of snow dug out his stick, which he'd lost in the morning and which had been lying in the gutter all day. He hadn't noticed it because he had been holding his head so high; nor had his men, who had also been bursting with pride. Now, as he walked along with eyes fixed on the ground, he spotted it at once. It must have fallen out of the streetcar when the refugees tripped over it during their arrival. It could be used as a walking stick. And that was what he did, because he was exhausted. But he also felt tormented, and hence ridiculous; and he was utterly mocked, and thus in despair, having been plunged into ridicule by a barely noticeable individual who had unexpectedly pulled himself from the depths of indignity. He had been able to do this only through a fierce tussle on the borderline between ridiculousness and despair. Because it is out of the despair of the ridiculous and the ridiculousness of the desperate that there arises such a change of roles; it is possible only when good fortune produces another character even more susceptible to ridicule. Self-love leads one to shun banality and secondariness, even if it means going it alone, even if it has to be at someone else's expense; and it makes one yearn for special means of expression – the firm tone, the disdainful glint in the eye, the supercilious pose – as if for one's own salvation.

The student still finds it hard to believe that a figure with no merits whatsoever to his name had, out of nowhere, become the commander of the guard. Could this possibly mean that promotion to commander of the guard meant nothing? Deprived not only of the gold braid but also of the guard that he himself had created, demoted by circumstance to a position even lower than the rank-and-file guardsmen, he had lost faith in his lucky destiny, and pride had gone out of him like the air from a pricked balloon. Alas, without faith and pride he was of no importance. There was no cause within view that he might take up, no place where his presence might still have any meaning. His high boots reminded him of events that aroused his repugnance, so he gladly left them on the mat outside the door, along with the remains of the stench that still clung to the soles. He pulled off his belt too. All he wanted now was to lock himself in his attic room. There he is, lying exhaustedly on the bedspread. From time to time he still belches from the lavish meal, but when hunger comes he will not find so much as a slice of bread at home. He lights a cigarette, his last one, and the air over the bed grows opaque with smoke. The student cocks his head and listens. Footsteps on the stairs stop at the floor below. So for the moment no one is coming for him. He would prefer it if later too it does not occur to the general to shut him up in the shelter beneath the cinema. But he does not know what he'll do with himself if he is left alone. He blows out smoke and stares through the window for such a long time it brings tears to his eyes. Outside is a clear sky cold as ice.

The residents of the apartment buildings willingly acknowledged that the resolute steps taken by the new leader with the rank of general exposed the underlying indecisiveness of the former leader with no military rank whatsoever, revealing his excessive scruples, his weakness for utterly civilian sentiments, and his lack of a sufficiently clear conception of what was proper and what was reprehensible. He had not been a true hero, prepared to do whatever it took to achieve an end that justified the means; this much was easy to admit after the fact. The first of the bold decisions by which the general showed he was a man of action was to keep the refugees in the shelter beneath the cinema, since they already happened to be there, standing in a crush just as they had stood earlier in the streetcar that brought them, as they waited for someone to let them out. If I am the general, I do not think especially highly of my idea, but I have to accept that for the moment no better one is to be found. Because even if, with an exceptional effort, the refugees were to be deprived of the property, so problematic for the public, that was their lives, little good would come of it – for what on earth was one then supposed to do with a quantity of useless bodies so great it made one's head ache? They would all still be sprawling about in that space, and their lifeless inertia would just make matters worse. There would be even more of a hurry to find a way out of an even more troublesome situation. In the general's view, leaving the refugees in the cinema was only a partial solution, though that alone was a great deal better than the timid procrastination seen thus far – than ducking the necessary steps – than relying on the benevolence of fate, in the hope that a solution would appear of its own accord. In the interests of order, all that needed to be done now was to round up the orphans.

Yet the hunt carried out noisily by the order guard was unsuccessful. The children were not found. They proved smarter than the guards; in addition, they had little to lose. The guardsmen captured only one little boy with mourning black on his sleeve and under his fingernails, and that by chance, as he was stealing sugar for his pals from some kitchen. Caught by the lady of the house and her neighbors, to begin with he fought like a wild animal, kicking and biting, till he ran out of strength. Later he allowed himself to be led to the general's staff, which was operating from the café at number one, and there, staring dully at the floor, he confessed to the clerk interrogating him that he had crawled through a window after removing the pane. The rest of his gang was stationed on the rooftops, serving under the command of a leader armed with a real revolver. For the information he had revealed, the boy concluded by demanding a bar of chocolate. If he had been questioned further, it might have come out that after the interrogation he expected to be set free.

It was his hope to return in glory to the roof, where he would distribute pieces of chocolate to those older than himself. The general ordered him to be locked up in the storage area behind the cloakroom. The notary, who was now participating in the work of the staff, heard the boy's statement. He went home to check in his drawer, and his worrying suspicion was immediately confirmed.

He had to inform his wife as soon as possible, so he waited for a single moment of quiet and calm – but in vain. In his apartment the storm raged unabated. His wife had quarreled with the maid about the chicken, the last wing from which had been given to the little girl when she woke from her long afternoon nap. A chicken had two lower quarters and two upper quarters. What had happened, then, to the carefully divided whole, of which three fourths were missing? As she conducted her investigation, the notary's wife was already partly aware of the scandalous truth. It had already come to her attention that the concierge had seen the policeman – who would have thought it, looking at that pudgy, lumbering maid – slipping out of the house down the service stairs, his uniform unfastened, a portion of chicken in his hand. It was not that three quarters of a chicken had gone missing, though that in itself was an absolutely unacceptable loss. The point, briefly put, concerned much more significant moral damage, things that one could not close one's eyes to, that were an offense to decency. The lady of the house had suffered terribly; her confidence had been abused and her home brought into disrepute. She did not have to tolerate vice under her roof a moment longer. She cared nothing for any other consideration; her conscience was clear.

But before the maid was given her notice, the son returned unexpectedly, frozen to the marrow, his nose and ears almost dropping off with cold, and with cracked glasses. When he appeared in the doorway the domestic argument, which had been going on since morning, dissolved temporarily in tears of relief. The lady and the maid spontaneously fell into one another's arms. Without wasting a moment, they lit the stove, heated the broth, and mixed up some egg yolks and sugar. The little girl came running in and clambered onto her brother's lap to warm his nose and ears with her sticky little hands. The notary, making a display of sternness, demanded the return of the revolver, which, however, proved impossible – the gun had remained on the roof, in the hands of the unpredictable newsboy from number eight, a notorious hooligan. All that could be done was to reassure the general that the chamber contained only a single bullet, as the notary knew best of all: he was keeping that bullet for himself, just in case he finally grew sick of life. One bullet was not a lot, but it was also far too much, since any person could be hit by it. For this reason the entire staff attempted to stop the general from acting; action seemed to all of them to be just as dangerous as inaction. In principle the loaded revolver ought sooner or later to be fired, though they were counting on the imperfect nature of the rules and the fact that from time to time they failed to operate. Maybe this rule too would not work – and even if it did, let it at least affect someone else. No one wished to part with life, including the notary, who had played the biggest role in bringing about the present situation and in fact was responsible for it. Each person had his own disagreeable notion of what might happen next. And because of all this no one knew what to do. To put an end to the disorder, a punitive expedition needed to be sent onto the roof. But the policeman had his own ideas; no longer young and carrying something of a belly, he preferred to announce over the megaphone that the newsboy's misbehavior would be forgiven and his morning fine annulled if he agreed to come down from the roof. Why would he not listen, having just a moment ago been betrayed by his friend? So long as he too had someone to betray, all was not lost.

And when the business was brought to a successful conclusion – when the tearful washerwoman took her recalcitrant son off to the basement of number eight, and the general got his hands on the revolver – at that moment the conspiracy of local and outside boys was finally broken up. What belonged here was once again separated from what had arrived from elsewhere, and this was the first step in coming to grips with the disorder. For all concerned it would have been safer if the gun had been returned to the drawer from which it was taken. But such a solution, incompatible with the general's will, was no longer possible. As for other matters, in the opinion of the guardsmen they were looking better and better. The children from the orphanage had nothing left to wait for, crouching half frozen on the roof of the government offices. They began waving a less than clean white handkerchief as a sign they had had enough. Held at gunpoint by the general just in case, they came off the roof one by one down the fire escape stairs into a circle of guards. Then, hands raised and eyes on the ground, in a huddled group they waited under escort in the middle of the square to see what would be decided in their case. Observed from a distance against the background of the grammar school coats – for example, from a window overlooking the street – even the tallest ones didn't seem so very big. Evidently not much was needed to put them in their place. The moment they began to get really cold they started to cower and sniff. If I am standing in the window, I believe that snuffling suits the orphans and matches their black armbands much better than running wild. The peaceful residents of the apartment buildings have a right to expect gazes fixed on the tips of shoes; they are entitled to count on quiet and humble behavior that does not clash inso- lently with the meaning of tight-fitting, frequently patched, threadbare little jackets. But in the question of the orphans, what on earth could be decided? They were taken to the shelter beneath the cinema, and that was all. There they could at last warm up, but on the other hand the crush was oppressive as they stood squashed between the overcoats of grown-ups. They could barely be heard as they whimpered about the lack of air.

If I am one of the residents watching from behind a lace curtain, the thought of the refugees locked up in the shelter does not worry me. Rather, I view everything as ending at its heavy door. The space that can be imagined on the other side doesn't even belong to this story. All I know is that the problem has ceased to exist, and the foreign body has been removed. The original state of affairs, which had lasted happily before the refugees arrived, has been restored. Having burst so obtrusively into the very middle of a familiar space that was neither large enough nor sufficiently well supplied for everyone, they had nevertheless finally been excluded from it, once and for all removed from the field of vision. What a relief it was for the residents. In this manner, before their very eyes, the story was heading towards an auspicious conclusion. Not a hair on anyone's head had been harmed and no one had suffered any wrong, aside from a few bruises and a certain amount of spilled blood.

In the meantime the row at the notary's house, which had died down for a moment, flared up again. Along with the return of the boy there had once more arisen the issue of the chicken quarters that before had not added up, and though the equation was finally balanced, the solution of the mystery led to further suspicions and further revelations. There was no end to the shouting. An answer was mercilessly demanded as to how the boy could have passed down the kitchen hallway unnoticed and then come back the same way carrying the pieces of chicken, the revolver under his jacket. Where was the maid at that time? Why was the door of her room closed? Faced with such insistence from the lady of the house, the son eventually revealed what he had seen through the keyhole as he had been creeping into the kitchen: a student cap casually thrown onto a stool. And since the matter had come up, he tried to say what he had heard as he paused outside the locked door, but he was interrupted. It was already too much. Enough to give the maid her marching orders just like that, without discussion. Things had to end with a dismissal. Because if it was no longer a matter of circumstantial evidence but of a certainty, and if it wasn't just the policeman but also the student, there was no knowing who else there had been. The maid would not say who else for anything. If that came out too – she had lost hope of being able to conceal anything at all – she would swear she had only been sewing buttons onto uniforms. The lady of the house was at a loss for words. Words were superfluous; all that was needed was to tip the contents of the maid's trunk onto the kitchen table under the lamp to make sure nothing would be stolen – and such a possibility had to be taken into consideration since she had not shown a shred of decency. But no object from the household was found in the maid's things – not even a certain silver spoon that had gone missing from its set a couple of days before. It was in vain that the lady of the house ordered the girl to turn out her pockets; there was nothing there either. After that she no longer knew where else to look. The matter of the spoon was of no consequence to the notary; because of the coup he had lost a great deal more, but since morning he had had time to come to terms with his losses, and by evening he was merely calculating what he still had. And his desires, like those mortally exhausted soldiers left in a hopeless position, were ready to surrender. When all of the maid's assets and liabilities had been scrupulously reckoned up, at the end the value of the silver spoon was subtracted. And what turned out was what was supposed to turn out – that she was not owed anything whatsoever.

Besides, the maid had no use for money – she would probably only have misused it if she'd been given it. She had been trying to save for her wedding, but who would marry her now that she had trampled her honor in the mud? If after all this she found employment anywhere at all without letters of reference, which the notary's wife was regrettably unable to provide, she would have board and lodging as part of her position. But without a job she was once again an outsider here. The day when the streetcar had brought her and her trunk so that, with advertisement in hand, she could apply for the post with the notary's family – that day continued to exist only in her imagination, like a calendar page lost among kitchen recipes, false by the very nature of things. The maid had no idea where she would go now. So she sat in the empty streetcar, with the same trunk as before on her lap, as if she still trusted that the streetcar would eventually move off and take her back where she had come from. But there was no return. Tears streamed down her face and froze on her cheeks. She sat there, expecting goodness knows what, till she grew cold. Then she asked the sentries of the order guard to let her into the shelter under the cinema. The sentries, with mock respect, opened the creaking door, from which there came a gust of stuffy air, then slammed it behind her again.

During this time other subordinates of the general were seeking in vain to establish who owned all the sacks of quick-lime, sand, and plaster that were stacked in piles in the auditorium of the cinema. Who had transported them there and who had unloaded them? Who had bought the cinema with a view to converting it into a quality fashion store with ready-made apparel? This was not known even to the general, though at one time he had been familiar with all the rumors circulating round the tables in the café. At this moment he was unable to resist an expressive gesture at the mention of the elegant store – a fluid motion of both hands evoking the suggestive idea of the female form, for he had already heard somewhere that the place was supposed to sell underwear. Women's underwear, that is. The general raised his thick eyebrows knowingly and gave a wink with the eye that was not swollen. That told his listeners everything they needed to know: corsets fastened with hooks and eyes, suspender belts, close-fitting winter woolens, cabaret slips in black and claret, brassieres with bows, and so on. When thinking of the aforementioned items of attire, guffawing was thoroughly appropriate.

But the general too was mistaken. Just as there had never been any cinema here, neither could there ever be such a store. The past into which the cinema had disappeared, and the future from which the store was supposed to emerge, can exist here only as crazy imaginings. The pages of the calendar, both those already torn off and those that remained, in their entirety possess less solid reality than exists on the painted plywood boards with their ostensible perspective. Since the owner of the sacks of quicklime was not found, the general, acting under conditions of emergency, requisitioned these unclaimed items so the order guard could make use of them. Once the initial decision had been made – to confine the refugees in the shelter – he did not hesitate to take the next step, which followed logically from the first. Doubts, fears, hesitations, cowardly attempts to involve others in troubling matters that a person ought to solve alone, like a man – such things were incompatible with the gleaming braid on the general's coat. To gain the respect of the public there was no need whatsoever to inform them of every step; quite the opposite, one should assume as much responsibility as possible, then lapse into firm and scornful silence. Once the worst has been overcome, a flash of braid is enough to allay various belated misgivings on the part of more delicate consciences. That was why the collar of the general's greatcoat was embroidered with gold thread. The young clerks from the local government offices, dazzled like everyone else, realized in the face of this brightness that their opinions were no longer needed. From that moment on they kept their mouths shut. They merely stood at attention, heels together, permanently ready to obey.

If I am the general, I have little to say to them. What's to be said here, when the situation is clear: there is a shortage of space. Why prolong the unnecessary suffering of stomachs laying claim to their dubious rights, the superfluous effort of lungs using air that was not theirs to breathe, or the futile beating of hearts filled with pointless resentment. Why consent to an existence that serves no worthwhile purpose but merely pays homage to the chaos of the transformation of material, the perpetual circulation of hope and despair, and in no respect, either figurative or literal, fulfills the requirements of orderliness. The general was calmly smoking a cigar he had found in the pocket of the greatcoat. Nothing had yet begun; for the moment the guards were only starting to bring buckets and spades borrowed from the concierges of the apartment buildings. The absolutely new idea for restoring order was a simple one. It required no preparations except the sealing up of a few ventilation shafts. Would the subsequent use of quicklime not be entirely advisable? The blotches of swirling fabric in every possible shade of dark blue and black would be swallowed up by a dirty white, which itself would then melt into darkness. Here and there a glint from house keys that had fallen from someone's pocket, or a vial of heart medication no longer needed. Blue and black are helpless when confronted with the grayness of the quicklime in which they are to dissolve. Between the sticky, caustic layers, bodies are forced to renounce utterly the space of their life. In that place it becomes evident that life is a joke and death has no meaning, rendered buoyant as it is by large numbers. Numbers make no impression on the general, because he knows his duty. A sense of responsibility necessitates extreme measures. The refugees are a separate matter. They will die and will forget everything. Their sufferings will vanish with them. No acrimony will poison the future. As they depart they will take with them their unconsidered opinions about what happened to them; they will be ill disposed towards those who remain behind, and filled with painful disillusion. They will take with them their resentment at not being able to demand compensation for their losses, forgetting that those losses were no one's fault. Without them the world will be better: cleaned of an accumulation of wrongs and reckonings, of distressing events and outdated cares, for a short moment it may even be capable of sympathy, close to a short-lived perfection, as if brand-new.

The general will not stop at anything, that much is sure. He seeks to carry out his duty conscientiously, then immediately to cast from his memory the details of what it fell to him to do. He would have found it especially intolerable to be called upon to explain his actions. But is he not afraid after all that at some point in the future some higher authority will take an interest in the matter of the shelter beneath the cinema? Perhaps someone will open it one day? Perhaps their spades will encounter the remains of fabric and padding, eaten away by quicklime? But what higher authority, for goodness' sake, and what future? The true nature of the highest authority is permanent absence. Besides, where would they come from, when here even the director of the local government offices is missing, and a few yards from the square the space is blocked off by city landscapes painted on sheets of plywood?

Now things must move faster, as the general too is in a hurry. Having already been derailed from its course, the story has entered on a different track. The same one that every story ends up on unavoidably sooner or later, because it is the track of the world, always ready to give direction to whatever is moving without purpose or destination. In the quiet of early evening, the story is already heading straight towards violent and cruel events, as if there were no one to take care of it. If this story belongs to me, I am powerless to change its course or turn things back. But insofar as I have any influence at all, this is the last moment to consign to oblivion all that the refugees spoiled with their incursion; to forgive them their inconvenient existence and their resulting tendency to occupy space; to justify the persistent efforts of these characters to disappear somewhere, the beating of their hearts, and the spasms of their defenseless stomachs. Things have gone so far that I have no other way out than to admit I belong to this crowd, and to shoulder the troublesome burden of affiliation. There is no escaping it.

The glow of evening heralds an approaching finale. It pulses beneath closed eyelids. The heavens will flame crimson until at some dark moment stars appear. It is only a certain quantity of silver nails, embedded in the fabric covering the vault and needed only to hold up the folds of satin, or rather of cheap, shiny sateen, the same material used in the linings of the overcoats. The nails have been hammered in firmly and permanently, yet all the same they can never be properly counted: they hide in the folds then wink mockingly from the edges first of one constellation, then another, proving that arbitrary boundaries mean nothing. The familiar names of groups of stars are nevertheless scrupulously listed on the invoices, without any reference to symbolic meanings: in the columns for amount and type of material, every metaphor is converted into small change. Does this mean that the stars are used only for successive, ever more artful abuses – that their very existence creates the groundwork for subterfuge? Are they otherwise unnecessary? Far from it. If the return of the silver nails were to be demanded in strict accordance with the invoice, there would be nothing to hold up the vast sheet of dark-colored fabric that is the lining of the sky. It would inevitably come fluttering down, revealing a structure of rough pinewood boards. But no one would even see it. The whole world would be thrashing about in the shiny folds, amid a fearful din of confused voices and scattered thoughts that would be lying everywhere like broken glass.

In the dingy warehouse the master craftsmen are calmly playing cards for a diamond necklace taken from the notary's safe; it lies on the table in an open velvet-lined box. No one is going to claim it now. They have no worries about their own business. All the principle installations are in their hands and all will continue to turn a profit for them. Only their perpetually smoldering anger at being condemned to a life without women suddenly ignites within them as they fling down a king on top of the queen of hearts. The masters regard their clandestine exploitation of the back area as their one and only privilege, barely sufficient compensation for the incomprehensible restrictions placed upon them; they will not stop at anything to protect it. Anyone who sought to prevent them would have to be prepared for the worst – for a mad escalation of losses, and destruction that can scarcely be imagined before it happens. It makes no difference to them whether anything remains intact, and the only thing they will insist on is the principle of having their own way. Anyone who cares about more than profits and losses, in turn, has to bend beneath their steadfast indifference, since in indifference lies strength, while in attachment there is only weakness. If this is my story, I am forced to negotiate, to accede to humiliating compromises, to make concessions, without losing hope.

From a certain point of view there are no made-up stories. Towards the end, all appearances to the contrary, each one turns out to be true and inevitable. Each one is a matter of life and death. Anyone who spends time in its unseen back area has to accept all the shared and ownerless pain it contains, spilling this way and that – because the channels through which it flows are all connected. It may be that every character curses the place that has fallen to his lot, certain of having been cheated. Events are followed with suspicion, like the questionable numbers popping out of lottery machines. But the more profound one's despair and doubt, the more powerful the belief that some almighty and impartial higher authority will render judgement, weighing wrongs and making amends for suffering. And if for some reason this is not possible? They would accept even bare-faced injustice and malicious disrespect more trustfully than helpless silence. If this is my story, they will forgive me all my transgressions. Helplessness alone will prove to be truly unforgivable, because it alone offends every one of the characters, upsetting their sense of purpose and wounding them by depriving them permanently of hope. As the ending approaches, there is no one left to take on the weight of all the failures and humiliations that were too much even for those most used to carrying them. If this tale belongs to me, at the present moment I merely squeeze my eyes shut so as not to see anything at all. Am I not the very last character of all here, the one who in the end must assume the entire pain alone?

As the conclusion of the tale draws near, the singing of guardsmen rises over the square. The singing calms anxiety and clouds thought. It brings a waking dream to the choir, and to the first floors and the balconies as well. While the guards keep singing, they dream of courage and of brotherhood unsullied by the filth of personal calculations. The songs have no power of their own but draw strength from the stillness. They are able to ring out so resonantly because the other sounds of the world have suddenly fallen silent. A sentry watching the door to the shelter pokes the snow sleepily with one of the walking sticks confiscated from the refugees. Let's say he happens to have been issued the white cane. Yet this is of no significance – there will not be any further occasion for him to use it to impose compliance. At some point he is bound to be surprised by the oppressive quiet in the place where previously there had been a muffled hum of voices. He cautiously opens the sealed entrance and looks into the cellar that his commander ordered him to guard. It is empty, completely empty from one end to the other; no one is there, though the air is thick with the smell of mothballs and breathing. The sentry cannot believe his eyes. He calls his comrades and his superiors, he calls the policeman, he runs to the general himself. Those who were confined there have vanished without a trace, even the children from the orphanage, even the notary's maid – yet the padlock on the door was untouched. Encircled by his staff, the general examines the padlock closely as an incomprehensible curiosity. Each person separately has the fleeting impression they are dreaming, for there is no other way to explain what they are seeing with their own eyes. But common sense is unable to rebel in the face of the evident.

Nothing can be reversed; what is done cannot be undone.

A disturbing sense of unease sweeps over all those involved, as if they suddenly felt someone's eyes on their backs just when they were sure that what they were about to do was no one else's business. They are immediately struck by some unspecified fear, even though they had already gotten used to other people being afraid of them. After all, everyone knows that only the dead pass no judgment and acquiesce humbly to everything. So now it must be accepted that an action which would in no way have offended the dead might well be denounced by the survivors. They cannot be expected to forgive it all easily: the deliberately sealed vent, the spades, and the sacks of quicklime prepared ahead of time. Their outrage, it would seem, broke free at the same time they themselves did; it will take an unpredictable course, and each of the guardsmen wonders where else it will lead.

At the general's request, the residents were questioned with regard to the disappearance of the refugees. But here too the inquiry ground to a halt. No one had seen a thing, though as the general kept repeating, and after him the policeman and the guards, it wasn't possible that so very many witnesses should have failed to notice the departure of such a large crowd. Then someone was lying, the general was forced to conclude, and someone perhaps was guilty of treachery. What if the treachery were to go unpunished; what if the guilty party avoided being unmasked and, even worse, stood there saluting the general with a click of the heels as if nothing had happened? Yet the details of this affair, the question of the unaccountable disappearance of so many people at once, baffled the minds of all those who attempted to fathom it. If this is my story, I will allow them to drop the matter, exhausted as they are by their futile inquiries, as a mystery that for them cannot be solved.

Evidence of the fleeting presence of the refugees has remained only in the pictures taken by the photographer. Here a little girl looks directly at the lens; only her eyes can be seen from behind the pillow she holds in her arms. Here people with empty jars form a line for water, snaking round the shut-off faucet; here the orphans in patched clothing reach for a basket of rolls, licking their lips in anticipation. In the background is the crowd, always the same, dragging their suitcases along and stooping under the weight, sitting on them, not allowing themselves easily to be separated from their belongings. If these people were asked their opinion now, they would surely agree that it would have been best not to take any luggage with them at all. But who could have known ahead of time, they would add with a shrug. They would not have liked the photographs taken on the square, where they had found themselves against their will and where their feelings had been trampled underfoot. For sure they would have wanted the photographer to destroy the pictures along with the negatives. If they had found out that, on the contrary, he intended to sell them for a handsome sum to certain astute press agencies, they would have been indignant. Seeking to prove that those pictures contained images taken out of context, false and of no value, they could have shown numerous private photos from their wallets, on which, it had to be admitted, they came out incomparably better. And the earlier pictures, in which they appeared in the fullness of their good looks, good health, and prosperity, would be a proper memento of them. Their eyes gazed into the future without a trace of terror; their clothing was brand-new and not yet disheveled by fate. This is what ought to have remained as their visiting card in the present story when they themselves had already left it. But from the very beginning the refugees' opinions were not consulted in any matter, and now that they are gone, they count for even less.

Alas, if someone had hoped that after their disappearance the frost would ease up or the guards would turn back into schoolboys, subsequent developments were to disappoint them. It was the armbands on the school coats that created the guards, and they are easier to put on than to take off. Now the threads of local stories, which in the view of the residents ought to have been the most important, had suddenly been snapped off at a random moment as if in themselves they were of no significance. The notary had managed to drag himself out of bed in the morning, but he had not even made it to his office. The policeman had begun his rounds but hadn't finished them. The maid had prepared lunch, but the family had not gathered round the table. After disposing of the remnants of the foreign story that had encroached on the local tale, the latter ought to have continued smoothly on. It would have been nice to believe that nothing had happened. Or that what had taken place was a transitory and inconsequential interruption in the course of more important concerns, such as family life, work, and secret passions. But the desired return to the point of departure ceased being possible when the story of the notary lost its original cohesiveness. After the obstacle that blocked its advance was removed, the story itself no longer had any meaning. This slackening off makes itself felt ever more acutely. The notary falls asleep in an armchair, and his desires yield to the forces of inertia, like the aforementioned soldiers wearied by a hopeless fight who finally leave their fortress under a white flag of surrender. The policeman, who from morning till evening has done everything he could, dozes off on a kitchen stool while the water cools in the basin in which he is soaking his corns. The singing stopped some time ago, but it still rings in the ears. The residents won't even notice when they drift into the sleep they emerged from in the morning. Bodies in one place, clothing in another – arranged tidily on hangers, and no longer needed here. An unbroken quiet will take over, like inside a glass ball in which, after a vigorous shaking, everything returns to its place.

In the meantime, however, the general is unable to regain his composure. What he ordered to be locked up should have remained so, period. The general is not fond of surprises, especially those that require additional explanations, because as a seasoned soldier he is well aware that additional explanations never make sense and serve only to pull the wool over people's eyes. All he can do is blame the sentries. The absence of the crowd is nothing but a special form of presence, and what has changed is in essence of secondary importance. Since the refugees are no longer here, they must be somewhere else, that much is obvious. But if such is the case, where are all those people now? Where is the woman in the white fur coat, where is the pair of newlyweds, their wedding outfits sprinkled with confetti? That the general does not know. Nor does he know where the schoolgirl in pigtails is, along with her elderly grandmother, who wanted all along just to sit down comfortably somewhere, nothing more; or the blind man with the violin in a case. And above all the family that in the confusion had lost its newborn baby. If the general wanted an answer from me to the question that was tormenting him, he might receive one, but he would not believe it. I close my mouth and will not say a word to the general. For sure? What if I am pressured? What if a peremptory command is issued, backed up with the irrefutable argument of a cold gun barrel on the back of my neck? I admit this would come as a shock. But even then, no. For the privilege of not opening one's mouth it is worth paying any price. To the very end there is hope, however slim, that resistance will triumph. That by some miracle the mechanism, imperfect by its very nature, will once again jam before the fatal click of the firing pin. As the story comes to an end only one thing is worth counting on: the failure of the rules, and a beneficent confusion that will blunt the inexorability with which effect follows on the heels of cause.

Baffled by the mystery without a solution, the general above all wants to know the truth. But the truth, long ridiculed and rejected, would now sound like a bad joke. Did it not circulate in its time in the form of a rumor about taxicabs that were supposed to come for the refugees and take them to a better place? At that time too it failed to convince the general. This is a sign that it is not meant for him. Yet it does exist. It declares that the refugees are now living in America. Even if it were not obvious why it should be America in particular, still the inquisitive residents would have no choice but to accept this fact. How the crowd got there is a more complicated affair, though at the same time, on the contrary, the simplest thing of all. The answer may be difficult or easy, depending on who I am.

So then, if I am the baby born at the wrong time – and could I be anyone else? – the answer is easy, and I know all there is to know about this matter. I'm thoroughly familiar with every detail and every expense associated with it. Everything here belongs to me: the glints of light on the windowpanes, the yellow of the plasterwork, the white of the clouds, the smell of soapy water, the heaviness of the basalt cobblestones. But there are only as many of these possessions as will fit in the heart and the mind. In order to communicate with the people carrying out the work, such things have to be converted into money – the rustling harmonies of banknotes. I use my slender means sparingly – they have to cover general costs like the decoration of interiors, and lighting, and the maintenance of the installations, not to mention the personal needs of notaries and their wives, children, maids, and concierges. And also of pharmacists, bakers, custodians, and clerks. And thugs smashing windows with sticks – even they must not be overlooked. And since the available resources are by the nature of things in short supply and there is not enough of anything to go around, the men in overalls are always disappointed by the scant possibilities for lining their own pockets on the side. Every story is ravaged by tensions; every one is destroyed by the flaw of contempt. Sooner or later someone who will end up paying for it all will come along. Whether I like it, or not, the homeless crowd, now dressed one way, now another, passes through every story that can be set in motion.

The nature of the whole is at fault; it knows no equilibrium. Paved with the best of intentions and propped up by the fractured dictates of conscience, the world in the end always begins to fall to pieces in one place or another. Every collapse turns out to be a catastrophe for someone; after each one, frantic cries for help fly one way or the other. The iron laws of acoustics render them inaudible. It is hard to renounce inattention, that sated, self-absorbed aversion to details. An overly close knowledge of things always entails obligations of some sort. I have to do all I can to open the emergency exits in time. As far as exact solutions are concerned, they are not complicated. All that is needed are a few steps and a section of corridor. A tunnel will be necessary for the taxicabs to get through. The masters, of course, can make one available, though they do not have to. Aside from the services listed in the invoices, I expect others from them of a confidential nature, out of courtesy. I acquiesce in every matter of lesser importance. Squirming with frustration, I turn a blind eye to botched work, underhand dealings, and impunity. I pay without making demands. I accept fraudulent accounts at face value, as long as they agree to open up their tunnels at the required time. Aware that I have no choice, the masters dictate the conditions.

The fallen angels of the back area hold themselves in high regard because of certain special talents they have picked up in the course of their perpetual machinations, as they chased around after small-scale profits and knowingly exploited the nature of things, which have a constant tendency to pass and be gone. For all their faults, the workmen excel at their trade. They have acquired to a fault the art of handling inanimate matter: they are casually able to combine it with nothingness, to mix what exists with what does not, to blend the one and the other into a homogeneous product, an indissoluble amalgam. Through the years of their nonchalant practice, constantly juggling with materials and invoices, they have achieved perfection. Without them neither the creation of America nor its upkeep would be possible. Matters of life and death depend on their idle and capricious good graces. Yawning, they do what is necessary, at the last minute, more worried about counting pallets and cases, because that is the only thing truly important to them. The back area has no room for pity or compassion.

A LONG MOTORCADE OF TAXICABS filing quietly along will appear at the end of this story. All the cabs are full. Slowly, rocking through the darkness on overloaded springs, they are driving straight to America. In this way the refugees finally end up in an earthly paradise, or perhaps a posthumous one – in this matter they will never be entirely sure. They find themselves at the feet of immense mansions made from their own dreams turned into stone, amid vertiginous skyscrapers and sleek towers that soar upward one next to another, their steel needles piercing the sky, with an unparalleled lightness, like all that the ground cannot control. Having miraculously survived, they gaze at themselves in mirrored windows and the glistening bodywork of limousines, dressed in used American clothing from Salvation Army stores. What became of the clothes made for them by the tailor? In those outfits salvation would have turned out to be as shabby as the clothes themselves. Those garments were failures from the start, of no use for anything. The tailor himself knows best how he cursed at them, so he will not miss them either. Now it is of no importance what happened to them. They may be moldering on an American trash heap, though it is more likely they were wedged in between layers of caustic quicklime, stiffened and burned through. In light-colored trench coats and hats pulled over their eyes, in striped pants, in backless dresses, elbow-length gloves, and feather boas, the new owners of this attire begin a new life, realizing they could no longer insist on the old life and the old clothing.

It would be most comfortable at this point to stop at the obvious advantages of such a turn of events, and resist any temptation to dig deeper. Especially not to inquire what all those people do in America, how they make their living, and what hopes they have. Even if it were the smallest America one could possibly have, made up of no more than a handful of skyscrapers and a few streets, maintaining this immense construction with all its wonders requires unbelievable sacrifices. The exorbitant costs incline one naturally to a simple-hearted optimism. It is not easy to accept a fiasco when such large investments are involved. Yet it's plain that America came from the same hands that bungled everything they touched. Hands that never missed an opportunity for a swindle.

Besides, the sequence of events has a perpetual tendency to stray from its anticipated course, and to yield to disconcerting complications. For example, the notary's maid, now with short hair and wearing lurid makeup, is to be seen every evening entering the brightly lit bar on the corner, toying with one of her long gloves. She sits on a bar stool, crosses her legs, and lights a cigarette in a long holder. She is not unhappy. The place is filled with music; its mirrors gleam and gold paint glitters everywhere. The men sprawling on the sofas are all lawyers, handsome young bachelors working in the firms of notaries and attorneys or the offices of judges. So she never complains, having her regular clients; and when one knows the whole picture, it's obvious she could not have found a better situation.

If other details were inquired into, it would transpire that the children from the orphanage support themselves by nighttime robberies; during an argument about a wad of green five-dollar bills, they wave switchblades at one another. But they never lack for American chocolate, the sweetness of which eventually assuages their anger; they have it in abundance, the regular sort or with flavored fillings, any kind they could wish for. It may also turn out that the woman in the white fur coat, now thrown on carelessly over her lingerie, has been forgotten, and is drinking to her reflection in a hotel mirror. But all she needs to do is take the elevator down to the casino and play the roulette wheel as many times as it takes, betting on the red or the black, for her to have everything one would expect in the dressing room of a famous artiste: fresh flowers, open bottles of champagne chilling in ice buckets, canapés with caviar brought in on a silver tray by the liveried bellhop. The blind man is likely playing his violin in second-rate restaurants, cheated by the cloakroom attendant night after night. But on sunny mornings the chords of his own compositions fill the entire space, capturing the ups and downs of life and giving them the meaning they lack; the silvery notes soar all the way up to the fantastical copings of the skyscrapers. The schoolgirl and her elderly grandmother are warming themselves in the sun on a little deserted square squeezed between the insurance companies and the banks; they always have every bench to themselves. The newlyweds have been involved in divorce proceedings for many years now, and meet only in the courtroom. The husband, his temples flecked with the first signs of grayness, is supposed to marry the beautiful daughter of an American millionaire. The wife is about to open a large store selling bridal wear; it's filled with dazzling white chiffon gowns with veils, and tuxedos black as pitch.

The mother of the family is tranquil, as if the injection she was given to calm her down never stopped working; the father is slaving to death on the production line of a huge auto plant. He wants to secure a better life for his ungrateful children than he himself has had. But the children are already hurtling recklessly towards their future calamities. This family alone has not been given a better fortune by America. Their grief was probably too great. They brought it with them, and though they do all they can to forget it, they cannot. The kind of pain that fell to their lot can never be eased by any medication, even death.

Happy endings are never happier than is possible. It might seem that, like a springtime thaw, they bring the promise of a new beginning, but the truth is otherwise. They merely lay bare the rotting matter of dashed hopes. Fortunate turns of events bring no relief, consumed as they are by the mold of unintentionally ironic meanings, and shot through with the musty despair of past seasons. And it is from them, these endings which end nothing, that new stories will grow.